OPERATION R.O.C

MATTHEW DENNION

SEVERED PRESS
HOBART TASMANIA

OPERATION R.O.C

To my beloved wife for watching hours of cryptid shows and the kaiju classic Rodan with me at least a dozen times!

PROLOGUE

The rain poured down from the night sky and drenched the marshy area of the Scape Ore Swamp in South Carolina. The gathered Thuggee cultists were soaked but they kept their vigil on the cave that they had discovered days ago. Their leader, the Rol-Hama, was the high priest of Kali. He was a large and powerful man standing at 6'5" and weighing over 250 pounds, with hardly an ounce of fat on him. Rol-Hama sat almost motionless staring into the opening of the cave. His eyes gleamed as if he was on the verge of attaining the most valuable treasure that he had ever seen. A bolt of lightning streaked across the sky, but despite the danger of being struck by the fire of the heavens, none of the cultists dared to enter the cave of the beast.

The creature in the cave was the last target on their list. Once Rol-Hama had captured the creature, the Thuggee would be able to begin their reign of terror in the name of Kali. Of all of the creatures that they had captured, this beast was the most difficult to locate due to the harsh environment of the swamp.

Legends of the reptile that walked like a man were as old as the human race, but the last verified sighting of a living beast man was only 5 years ago. Several months ago, the Rol-Hama had instructed his followers to begin searching the swamp. Their search finally paid off, when two days prior, several of his followers had discovered the unmistakable spoor of the monster. Once they had found the initial spoor they narrowed their search to an area roughly 10 miles wide. The cult then searched from the perimeter of the designated area inward until they had reached their current location. The spoor of the man-monster was dispersed around the cave, leaving no doubt that it was the lair of the creature.

The cultists were too cautious to enter the cave and meet the monster in its own domain. Rol-Hama had ordered that camp be set up near the mouth of the cave, where the cultists would wait for the monster to hunt once more. The beast had not eaten in days, and Rol-Hama was certain that the creature would leave its lair soon. No sooner had the thought crossed the Thuggee priest's mind then something started to move in the cave. Rol-Hama stood, and with emphatic but silent gestures, he ordered his men into position around the cave.

The monster cautiously exited its lair. It had no sooner stepped into the rain than a net was tossed around it. The creature thrashed violently.

Rol-Hama screamed for more ropes to be wrapped around the beast. A cultist ran toward the creature, with a rope in his hand, but as he approached the monster, the man-beast had managed to free its head from the netting which encircled it. The monster sprang forward and sank its fangs into the cultist's throat. The beast held its grip on the victim as more cultists continued to wrap ropes around it. When the creature saw more of the humans coming to him he tossed the corpse of his first victim aside, and his jaws shot forward and closed around the skull of a second cultist. The cultist's head exploded like a ripe grape under the tremendous pressure being exerted on it. With a speed that defied belief, the scaled leg of the creature shot out, and the talon at the end of it sliced open the stomach of another cultist. The cut was so fine that the cultist did not even realize that he had been injured until his intestines spilled out of his gut. Despite that fact that three of his followers had met a horrible death, Rol-Hama screamed in excitement. The creature was deadlier than he had ever imagined. Even when entrapped in a net and bound with ropes it was still able to slay some of the most skilled warriors on the planet with a single blow. After a long struggle, the creature was finally brought to the ground.

Once the beast was forced to the ground it began to thrash with even greater ferocity than it had when it was standing. At Rol-Hama's command, several cultists removed dart guns and began firing tranquilizers into the creature. Dozens of darts struck the creature and still it struggled with the same ferocity that it had at the inception of the battle. The creature's durability had confirmed for Rol-Hama that he had made the right decision to entrap the creature before attempting to tranquilize it. Had they simply fired darts into the creature it would have fled into the swamp, and precious more weeks, if not months, would have been wasted tracking the creature once more. The cultists fired several hundred darts into the creature before it finally began to slow down and eventually pass out. The creature had managed to slay five more cultists before it finally succumbed to the drugs coursing through its system.

When the creature had completely passed out, Rol-Hama walked up to the subdued beast and laughed manically. He then turned to his remaining followers. "Fellow sons of Kali. We have completed the first part of our sacred mission. We have captured the last of the monsters which we require to create our army. The legendary Lizard Man is finally our prisoner! We shall return to our lair, where he shall be transformed into a warrior of the will of Kali. With this creature and the other beasts that we have captured, the entire world will soon accept Kali as the one true God or they shall perish under the feet of her soldiers."

A loud chorus of cheers answered Rol-Hama as he stood over the unconscious Lizard Man. In the deranged mind of Rol-Hama, he could hear the cheers of his followers slowly changing to the screams of the non-believers. The people of Earth did not believe that Kali existed. They did not believe that the Thuggee existed, and most of all, they did not believe that the creatures which haunted the fringes of their society existed. Rol-Hama knew that all of these things existed and that they all wielded great power. He also knew that soon the world would be aware of their power as the blood of the non-believers washed away the misconceptions of the old world in preparation of the coming of Rol-Hama, the prophet of Kali.

Chapter 1

Atlantic City, New Jersey
Doug sat at the Blackjack table where he had just split two tens and was hoping to double his chances of walking away from the table in the positive. He was already up two thousand dollars, and his girlfriend, Kelly, had cautioned him several times just to take the two grand and walk away. Doug wanted to turn that two grand into four grand, and then enjoy the rest of their weekend in the city by the sea. Kelly was gripping his arm hard, and he knew that if he misplayed this double down that it would be a double loss. Not only would he lose his two grand but Kelly would nag him about losing the money all weekend. Doug figured that he could always regain the money later but losing an entire weekend to arguing and "I told you to walk away" could not be gotten back.

The dealer handed Doug his first card—the king of hearts. Doug shook his fist in triumph knowing that he would at least walk away from this hand ahead of where he was a few moments ago. The dealer placed the second card on his other ten to reveal a nine. Both hands were good enough to beat the dealer. Doug gave out a loud *yes*. Kelly screamed in joy and kissed him.

Doug took his chips and walked away with a huge smile on his face from the table over to the cashier, where he turned his chips into cash. Kelly was latched onto his arm as the couple walked out onto the boardwalk. It was a hot afternoon, but the wind blew a cool breeze from off the ocean onto the boardwalk. The sun was just starting to set to the west of the city, and it cast an orange glow onto the ocean. Doug was watching the sunset when Kelly grabbed him by the face and kissed him passionately. They had just started kissing when Doug pulled away from Kelly. She was aggravated at Doug, but he failed to notice the look on her face because his eyes were fixed on the setting sun and the odd shape silhouetted in front of it. Kelly started yelling at Doug when she too noticed the strange shadow heading for the city.

Doug grabbed Kelly's hand. "What the hell is that? Some kind of big-ass bird like a bald eagle or something?"

Kelly shook her head. "That's way too big to be a bird, but I can see its wings flapping, so it sure as hell can't be a plane either."

As the object flew closer to the city the couple could make out leathery bat-like wings and long goat-like legs that ended in cloven hooves. The creature had a powerful human-like torso with demonic claws instead of hands. The creature had a horse-like face with long curved horns on top of it.

Doug and Kelly had both grown up in New Jersey. They had both heard the legends of the beast that stalked the woodland area known as the Pine Barrens, but they had always assumed that the story was nothing more than a local legend or folktale. It was Kelly who first said the creature's name out loud, "It's the Jersey Devil."

Doug continued to stare in awe at the creature as it approached the city. "The Jersey Devil is supposed to be, like, seven feet tall. That thing is the size of a passenger plane."

Several other people on the boardwalk had noticed the approaching figure, and many of them were staring at the beast as it flew with the setting sun behind it and unleashed an ear splitting roar that shook the boardwalk.

A moment later, the giant Jersey Devil landed next to the Trump Taj Mahal. The creature towered over the structure. It roared once again, and then began smashing the once illustrious casino to rubble.

Doug and Kelly watched as police came running onto the boardwalk where they fired their useless guns and rifles at the kaiju. The monster ignored the bullets and finished destroying the Taj Mahal before heading to the next casino.

Kelly screamed, "We have to get out of here!" She began running down the boardwalk.

Doug grabbed her and started pulling her toward the beach. "We have to get clear of the buildings! Debris is falling on the boardwalk!"

Kelly briefly turned around to see a large chunk of concrete fall onto an elderly couple trying to flee from one of the casinos. She shivered and then focused on getting to the beach.

Doug pulled her to the very edge of the water so that they were as far away from the tall buildings as possible. Doug and Kelly stood at the water's edge as hundreds of more people followed their lead and ran as far away from the boardwalk as possible. Soon thousands of people were standing in ankle deep water as they watched the setting sun outline the horrific form of the demonic figure while it crushed building after building. Doug was sure that thousands more people were being killed inside of the buildings, and he was thankful that he was unable to hear their cries.

It took the Jersey Devil less than ten minutes to completely destroy seven different casinos and a large portion of the boardwalk. The creature stood in the rubble it had created when it turned its gaze toward the beach and roared.

As the sun outlined the kaiju, Doug could see why it was called the *Jersey Devil,* because it looked like Satan himself was standing in the wreckage of Atlantic City.

The gathered people standing in the surf shrieked in fear. They were trapped between a bloodthirsty kaiju and the Atlantic Ocean.

Doug grabbed ahold of Kelly's hand, and he began running down the beach. Their progress was slow as their feet sunk and slipped in the wet sand.

In two strides, the Jersey Devil had cleared the entire beach and had made his way to the water. He reached down with his claw at the mass of people below him. Dozens of people were impaled on his long claws.

Kelly looked back quickly enough to see the creature bring his claw up to his mouth where he closed his jaws on the screaming people. Kelly screamed in terror as she tried to pick up speed on the wet sand.

The Jersey Devil stepped forward crushing hundreds of people before his claw swept through the panicked mob, where he skewered more people on his claws before placing them in his mouth.

Doug pulled Kelly forward as fast as he could. They could hear the screams behind them and feel the beach shake with each step that the monster took. They had run only a few more steps when Doug heard Kelly cry out in pain. He turned around to see the end of a claw burst out of Kelly's chest and embed itself in his stomach. He was in unbelievable pain, but when he saw the fear in Kelly's eyes, he knew that he had to act.

He grabbed her hand as they were being lifted into the air. "Kelly, look at me! I love you, Kelly! I love you! Just keep your eyes on me—it will all be over soon!"

Kelly squeezed his hand as hard as she could. She saw a final glimpse of the setting sun before everything went black. She felt a brief surge of pain before her body finally gave out.

Doug lasted a few seconds longer than Kelly had. He held onto her hand as long as he could before he was tossed around the monster's mouth. He heard a loud scream of someone next to him followed by a crushing sensation, and then his pain ended as well.

CHAPTER 2

San Jose California

A light rain fell on the city causing steam to rise off of the hot streets. The steam was swirling as the light changed, and it allowed a group of people who had just exited the subway system to cross the street and start on their journey home from work. Brian Diggs was in that crowd, and after a difficult day of laying people off from his company, he was anxious to get home and try to de-stress. Because he had been so busy at work, he was not up on the news of the day. He was scanning the news feed on his phone and saw some kind of report about a devil attacking Atlantic City. He was still reading the report when he turned the corner to his street, and a horrible odor overwhelmed his olfactory senses. He looked up from his phone and down the street. "Holy God, that smell is awful! What the hell is that?"

Apartment windows began to open on both sides of the street that Brian stood on. People walked by wafting their hands in front of their faces as they turned curious gazes in search of the source of the stench. A man looked at Brian, and asked, "What is that smell?"

Brian shrugged when the entire street suddenly shook underneath of him. Brian and everyone else feared that it was an earthquake, but the shaking quickly stopped. A moment later the ground shook again, and the thought of an earthquake was still at the forefront of everyone's mind. Brian took out his phone and began dialing 911. Even if this was a small earthquake it could have ruptured a gas line, that could account for the odor. When Brian received a message that *All operators were currently busy* he was sure that an earthquake had struck the city. That would explain why so many people were calling for help. The street shook again as several of the cars on the city street bounced up and down. This time the shaking was followed by a guttural howl that

Brain thought reminded him of the sounds that the chimpanzees made on the show he watched on the Nat Geo station last night.

At this point, the street was filled with people. They were all walking in the direction of the smell and the howl. Brain had no idea what was going on. He knew that this part of town was pretty far from the zoo. There was a veterinary hospital nearby. Brian mused that perhaps a monkey or chimp was being treated there, and in the confusion of the quake, it had escaped. Brian was at the back of the quickly growing mob as it slowly plodded down the street. The street shook again, and there was another howl when out of nowhere a gargantuan figure stepped into view.

Brain looked in awe at the titan standing before him. At a quick guess, Brain figured that the monster was over two hundred feet tall. The creature was bipedal with a human-like build to it, except that even for its size its shoulders and arms were huge. The creature was covered from head to toe in a dark brown matted fur, and it quickly became apparent that the odor filling the street was coming from the creature. The street was full of people standing completely still and staring at the creature—their minds trying to comprehend what they were looking at.

It was Brain who first said the word, "Bigfoot?" aloud. Almost in response to Brain's supposition, the kaiju roared and then charged down the street.

The people closest to the creature were crushed under its aptly named big feet as the Sasquatch ran them down. In addition to crushing people under his feet, the monster was striking out at the buildings causing debris to fall onto the people who he did not crush directly.

Brain and the rest of the mob turned and began to run away from beast. Brain knew that they could never outrun the monster. He took the only option available to him as he silently began to pray for help from above.

Brain's prayers were answered as three military-style helicopters descended from above and were slowly hovering at the opposite end of the street from the Sasquatch. The monster was still crushing people and pounding on buildings when the helicopters opened fire with their high powered machine guns. Brain and countless other people spread to the sides of the street and pushed into the doors of any building that they could find entrance into.

Brain dove into a grocery store where he covered his ears to shield them from the sounds of the horror taking place outside. He watched in disbelief as the Sasquatch walked through the barrage of bullets from the helicopters. Brain was talking to himself as his mind was trying to process everything that he witnessed. "Not only is Bigfoot real, but he is an indestructible giant?"

Brain watched as the Sasquatch moved with speed that defied belief as he sprinted toward the helicopters. Dozens more people were crushed under the monster's feet. He continued to stare at the monster as it swatted the helicopters from the air as if they were nothing more than flies sent to annoy him.

Within seconds, the battle was over. Brian was left staring up at the enraged Sasquatch as it roared at the smoldering wreckage of the helicopters before it. Brain shook with fear, thinking that he was next, until the Sasquatch began pounding on the building across the street from him. While Brain prayed for the people in that building he was relieved that dumb luck had finally smiled his way. He began to think that the monster would destroy that building, and then hopefully continue down the street. That would allow Brian to slip out into the desolation and make his way to a home that he prayed was still intact. A small smile crept onto Brian's face but it was quickly replaced with a shriek of terror as the Sasquatch turned and began to vent its anger on the building that Brain was hiding in. The last thing that Brian saw was a bigfoot hovering in front of him as the roof collapsed and killed him instantly.

CHAPTER 3

Air Force One

The President sat in the situation room of Air Force One with members of his cabinet: the directors of Homeland Security, The CIA, The FBI, and high ranking officials from all branches of the military. The President addressed the assembled individuals, "All right everyone, I want to take one more look at this video. I want complete silence as we view it, and then I want your thoughts on how the United States can address this predicament both at home and abroad."

The President pressed a button on his tablet, and the screen at the far of end of the situation room came to life. A muscular man with tanned skinned appeared. The President thought that if it were not for the man's shaved head that he would have sworn that the man was actor/wrestler Dave Bautista.

The individual looked grimly into the camera for a long minute, and then he finally started speaking. "People of Earth, I am Rol-Hama, leader of the Thuggee and supreme priest of all powerful Kali. For too long, the ignorance and lethargy of non-believers has dominated the destiny of the human race." Rol-Hama screamed, "This dominance ends now! For years, you have all operated under the assumption that Thuggee and Kali herself did not exist. This same arrogance and lethargy has led you to dismiss the reports of various creatures which lurk in the areas just outside of what you call civilization. Like the Thuggee these creatures know how to hide from you, how to remain invisible. You have mounted half-hearted expeditions to find these creatures, but just as you lack the conviction to apply discipline to your lives, you lack the discipline to locate these creatures."

Rol-Hama's voice returned to a normal volume, "As followers of Kali the Thuggee have the discipline and the conviction required to locate these creatures. We have spent decades tracking and capturing many of the creatures which you thought were imaginary and labeled as cryptids. These creatures have survived despite mankind's destruction of the planet, because they are both cunning and powerful. Through our advancements in science, and through the power of all mighty Kali, we have altered these creatures to an enormous size and augmented their already considerable strength, speed, durability, and endurance. These cryptids are now what popular movies would label kaiju." He paused for a moment to let his next words gain extra meaning, "Earlier today we unleashed two of these creatures onto specific targets in the United States. As the citizens of those cities and the U.S. military have learned, these creatures are not only extremely powerful and impervious to conventional weapons, but they are completely under our control."

Rol-Hama began screaming again as he laid out the demands of his plan, "We have more of these creatures waiting to attack cities in countries all over the world! Our demands are as follows: Each and every country shall agree to allow followers of Kali to assume leadership roles in their governments, where their society shall be reformatted to live in accordance with the wishes of Kali. For every day that at least one country holds out from accepting these demands, a monster shall attack a city." Rol-Hama smiled. "You must all learn to live in unity under the direction of Kali, so you must all convert as one. If even one country holds out from our demands, then not only cities in that country, but cities all over the world will continue to feel our wrath, until the country which resists us yields to our demands." Rol-Hama smiled again. "You see, our kaiju will not only attack you directly, but they will force the rest of the people of the world to turn against you as well." Rol-Hama stared into the camera. "The next series of attacks will occur twenty-four hours from the release of this video. I suggest that the leaders of the world's soon to be former nations begun to discuss how to transition power to the Thuggee!"

The screen changed to a sign of the death goddess Kali. The President turned off the screen and addressed the situation room, "Gentlemen, it seems that we face a terrorist threat of a magnitude that we obviously never dreamed possible. We have a multitude of topics that we need to cover here and now. First, who is this Rol-Hama, and who or what are the Thuggee? Second, what do we know about the creatures that attacked Atlantic City and San Jose? Third, how are we going to combat this threat?"

George Mackenzie, Director of the CIA, stood up. "We currently have no information on Rol-Hama himself. The Thuggee are a group of assassins that have connections to both Hindu and Muslim cultures. This particular group seems to have ties to the cult of Kali. The Thuggee were thought to have been destroyed by the efforts of one Captain William Seelman in the early 1800s, but obviously they somehow managed to either hide in obscurity or they have recently reformed themselves."

Mackenzie brought up several images of Atlantic City, including the hellish image of the Jersey Devil standing in the wreckage of what was once a casino. "This is the image of the kaiju that destroyed Atlantic City. The beast seems to match one of the descriptions of the so-called Jersey Devil. We have no official information on the creature, but reports suggest everything from a possessed thirteenth child of a witch, to a demon from Hell, to a winged monster of some sort. Whatever it is, the creature left the city in ruins and then disappeared into the nearby forest. We currently are unable to locate the beast."

He then brought up images of the giant, hairy creature that had attacked San Jose. "These are the images from San Jose. As you can see, San Jose was also destroyed." The image of massive ape-like creature could be seen savagely attacking a building. "This creature appears to be a giant version of one of the more well-known cryptids. The creature is known as the Bigfoot or Sasquatch. This creature tore down dozens of buildings with its bare hands, and was able to withstand high powered gunfire at close range, before also disappearing into the forest."

Mackenzie looked directly at the President. "We do not know how the Thuggee captured these creatures, managed to get them to grow an enormous size, become seemingly indestructible, or gain control of them. The term Rol-Hama used, *kaiju*, means *mysterious beast* in Japanese. The term would seem to be an accurate description, because we have no idea what we are dealing with in regards to these creatures. We don't know how many of these creatures that the Thuggee have, where the kaiju are located, or where they will attack next."

The President leaned back in his chair. "That's an awful lot of bad news, Mr. Mackenzie. Is there anything that you do know about the situation?"

Mackenzie nodded. "Yes, sir. We know how we are going to respond to this threat." Mackenzie brought an image onto the screen that showed a massive domed structure that looked like a football field that was ten times larger than it needed to be. "We call this structure the *Nest*. It is located in central Kansas, it is our current destination, and it currently houses one of our top secret experimental projects known as *Project Thunderbird*."

An image of a huge bird easily three hundred feet tall filled the screen. The bird had an abnormally long neck and a face that looked almost reptilian in nature. The bird's feathers seemed out of place. The feathers looked almost as if they were non-organic. Mackenzie immediately began explaining what the program was and how it could combat the current threat, "This is one of subjects for Project Thunderbird. It is a combination of genetic engineering and cybernetics. Several years ago we found the skeletal remains of a large creature that seemed to be one of the missing links between dinosaur and bird. We called them *Thunderbirds* after the Native American legend of a giant bird. The remains of the Thunderbird were much larger than any of the remains of winged reptiles that we had discovered so far. The remains were about half the size of the current model on this screen. Using condors to carry the eggs, we were able to clone several of these Thunderbirds from the remains of the original. Through the introduction of a growth serum that used radiation, hormones, steroids, and through a process of selective breeding five generations removed from the original clones, we were able to create a generation of four birds between two hundred and fifty and three hundred feet tall."

Mackenzie took a brief sip of water before continuing with his presentation. "These Thunderbirds were further enhanced with cybernetic upgrades to make them the most advanced surveillance and quick-strike option in our arsenal. These birds have the ability to reach speeds in excess of Mach 6 at high altitudes, and they are equipped with the latest in stealth technology. They are undetectable by radar, and they have advanced surveillance cameras embedded in their eyes." He brought another picture onto the main viewing screen showing the cybernetic components of the bird. "The birds have several offensive capabilities as well. Since they were designed for quick strikes that could not be easily tracked to the U.S., the birds have no heat based weapons. So, no missiles or bullets that would be easy to identify with infrared satellites. They are extremely strong. In addition to the birds' naturally powerfully body, the muscles in their necks, beaks, wings, and legs are enhanced with hydraulic lifts. These birds are capable of lifting a nuclear submarine clear out of the ocean. The birds' necks also each hold two one hundred gallon liquid nitrogen tanks that they can spray from their mouths, with a range of up to five hundred feet. Lastly, the birds' feathers have been replaced with titanium blades coated with laser cut diamonds. The birds are able fire these feathers, and because of the diamond coating, they are able to shred through a destroyer as it if was paper. Theses feathers will be able to pierce the hide of any creature that we send them against."

Mackenzie then brought up a picture that looked like the headset to a gaming system. "The birds are influenced by a pilot who sends directions to the bird via brainwaves from this transmitter, to a receiver implanted in the bird's brain. The bird itself is a living, thinking cybernetic organism. The pilot can give the bird directions, such as where to fly, and when to utilize its weapons systems, but the bird has control over its moment by moment actions. For example, if our pilot directed the bird to attack one of the cryptids that recently attacked us, the pilot would determine when to utilize the detachable feather blades and freezing spray, but the bird would assume control of its actions in close quarters combat situations. We purposely programmed the birds this way for two reasons. First, because the bird is far more accustomed on how to utilize its body than our pilots are. The second reason is because a bird's reaction time is three times as quick as human's reaction time is in a flight or fight situation. So when it comes to clawing and biting against a target, we want the bird to control its movements and attacks."

Mackenzie could see a little trepidation on the face of the President and several other men in the room. Mackenzie quickly moved to quell their fears. "Even in close quarters situations the pilot would have the ability to direct the bird to fly away from a target and then re-engage."

Mackenzie took a deep breath. "Mr. President, we currently have four of these birds with pilots, who have being flying them for several weeks on field tests. These birds and their pilots represent our best option for responding to new kaiju attacks quickly and with as few civilian casualties as possible. I propose that we change project Thunderbird to Operation R.O.C.— Retaliation on Cryptids."

The President nodded. "Creative name with the ROC being the giant bird of mythology. You have convinced me on the ROCs. Now tell me about who our pilots are."

CHAPTER 4

The pictures of three men and two women filled the screen. Mackenzie began to review the biographies of each of the individuals who would be responsible for piloting the ROCs against the cryptids. Makenzie started by bringing up the picture of the squadron leader. The picture of a man who looked like a muscular version of Jimmy Hendrix appeared on screen. "Our lead pilot is Tobias Crow. Captain Crow is a member of the Air Force who has flown over twenty successful missions as a fighter pilot. Five of those missions involved instances where he landed behind enemy lines, and with a small group of individuals, infiltrated and destroyed a terrorist base of operations. He will piloting ROC One."

The picture of a young redheaded woman was next to come onto the screen. "The pilot of ROC Two is Captain Lindsay Munroe. She has the highest scores for both tactics and in air simulations in the history of the Air Force. She is young, at only twenty-one, but she is the most promising young pilot that our country has to offer."

Mackenzie followed with the other female team member by bringing up the picture of a middle-aged African American woman. "Captain Sheena Green is the senior member of our team. Captain Green flew nearly thirty successful missions for the U.S. Navy before she was shot down over Iraq. She suffered physical injuries that prevented her from being an active military pilot. She still has one of the best minds and instincts of any pilot in the military, so when the opportunity was presented to her to still fly active missions from the inside of a building, she jumped on it. She will be the pilot of ROC Three."

The next pilot was a young man with blond hair and blue eyes. "ROC Four will be piloted by Captain David Bixby. He has more confirmed kills of enemy pilots than any other pilot in the U.S. armed forces. He is a little cocky, but he is more than good enough in the air to have the right to be cocky."

Mackenzie brought a globe up onto the screen. "Mr. President, the current threat spans the entire planet. Without considering the use of nuclear weapons as an option, we are the only country with the capabilities of facing these cryptid kaiju attacks. Rol-Hama has suggested that he will try to pit countries against one another. Securing the United States only to have other countries that cannot defend themselves turn against us will be giving Rol-Hama exactly what he desires. I suggest we take a proactive stance against his campaign by contacting other nations around the world and asking them if we can house one of the ROCs at a spot that will allow it to cover a given part of the planet. This will allow us to use a ROC to combat a cryptid that is attacking a city within its protective zone in almost any part of the world."

Four red dots appeared on various spots around the globe. "I suggest we house ROC One in Texas. This will give us the optimal position to protect both North and South America. The cities at the farthest northern and southern points of both continents will be out of reach, but we suspect that the cities on both the U.S. East and West coasts will be the primary targets." The image of the globe next shifted to North Africa.

"If we position ROC Two in Morocco, we will be able to protect most of Europe, and many of the major cities in Africa as well." Next the globe spun to reveal Asia. "ROC Three will be positioned at the border of Russia and China. This will allow us to cover most of the major cities in China, Russia, and India. Asia is big and large parts of it, including Japan, will be unprotected in this scenario."

Next the globe spun to Australia. "ROC Four will be positioned in Australia, allowing it to protect the entire continent and parts of southern Asia. Given enough advanced warning ROC Four may even be able to protect the southern tip of Japan."

Mackenzie returned the screen to a picture of the Nest. "The good news is that even with the ROCs positioned around the planet our pilots will be able to control them from right here in the Nest. The feed they receive through the cameras embedded in the ROCs' eyes will function in real time." Mackenzie returned to his seat as he concluded his presentation on a response to the crisis.

The President was silent for a minute as he gathered his thoughts before responding. "The plan seems solid, Mr.

Mackenzie, but I would like to see these ROCs and their pilots before I start calling foreign countries and asking them to let us put a giant monster bird that we control right in their backyards."

Mackenzie nodded, and then pulled out his phone. "This is Director Mackenzie, please ask the pilots to have the ROCs descend to a cruising altitude and bearing that will bring them parallel to Air Force One."

The President stared at Mackenzie for a minute, and then alerts started blaring all over Air Force One. A secret service member ran up to the President. "Sir, we have four large identified craft approaching Air Force One. They do not appear on radar, but the pilot reports visual confirmation of the targets."

The President remained calm and asked that the window shades be opened so that he could see these objects. He looked out the window on the left side of the plane and saw two of the largest creatures that he had ever beheld. They were two massive birds each far larger than a blue whale, with shining metal feathers. The President looked out the right side of window and saw the exact same spectacle. He turned to Mackenzie. "How long have the ROCs been following us without Air Force One being able to detect them?"

"They've been flying above us and out of the pilot's view for the past half hour. As I said, they are equipped with the latest in stealth technology. Even the advanced security systems of Air Force One are unable to detect them."

The President nodded. "I am adequately impressed with the ROCs. Give the pilots the commands to have them start flying to the destinations that you have flagged. I would still like to land and talk to the pilots before calling the leaders of the other nations."

Mackenzie nodded. "Yes, sir. We will be landing at the Nest within the hour where you can meet the pilots. You will have plenty of time to talk them before the ROCs reach their targeted destinations."

Forty minutes later, Air Force one had landed at the Nest. Mackenzie led the President into the building. Most the building was a massive aviary where the ROCs lived and were cared for when they were not in operation. The President was finally taken to a small command center in the center of the building where he saw the four pilots sitting in what looked like recliner chairs, with virtual reality helmets over their heads. There were two women processing data from various computer screens that were set up around the pilots.

The two women continued to work as Mackenzie walked up behind them and introduced them to the President. He first pointed to a blonde woman, who despite being in her mid-to-late forties, was still very attractive. "Mr. President, This is Dr. Jillian Crean. She is the lead bio-engineer on this project. She was the woman who engineered the ROCs both genetically and mechanically."

Dr. Crean kept her gaze fixed on her computer. "Good morning, Mr. President. Please forgive me for not standing up, but the ROCs are at a critical point in their mission. This is the farthest that they have ever flown from the Nest, and I need to make sure that they are functioning at optimal capacity."

When Mackenzie walked over to the second woman, she stood at attention. "This is Dr. Tracy Curry. She is the genius behind the neuro-link system that connects the pilots with the ROCs."

Tracy smiled. "It's an honor, Mr. President."

The President shook her hand. "Dr. Curry, are you confident that the pilots will be able to stay connected with the ROCs over the extreme distances that we are going to have them operating from?"

Tracy nodded and smiled again. "Yes sir, Mr. President. We are able to connect video game systems that people can play with each other from across the planet in real time with an artificial environment that needs to be constantly updated around them. Compared to that, taking information from the real world and interfacing it with our pilots is a breeze."

The President nodded. "Playing games is one thing, but are you sure that the link with the ROCs will maintain its continuity? Having one of those giant birds go AWOL and attacking a foreign nation would not help the current situation."

Tracy directed the President to the feed on her monitor. "The link will hold, sir. We have run numerous simulations and our projections show that the link would hold as far away from the Nest as the moon, if the ROCs were capable of flying through space."

"Very Impressive. Now what about the pilots? Will I be able to speak to them as they pilot the ROCs?"

Tracy shook her head. "Give them a few more minutes to set the ROCs' flight patterns. Once the ROCs have their bearings the pilots will be able to disengage from controlling them until they are closer to their destination. If there is an issue with the ROCs prior to reaching their destination, Dr. Crean and her support team will quickly alert the pilots, who can then re-engage with their assigned ROC."

The President looked back at the four pilots as they disengaged from their neuro-link helmets. Captain Crow was the first pilot to walk over the President. The seasoned pilot saluted the President and stood at attention. The President returned the salute. "At ease, Captain. Everyone I have talked to so far has assured me that the ROCs will work just fine in response to the crisis we are currently facing. Still, I would feel better to hear how one the pilots feel about how the ROCs will respond during this crisis."

Crow spoke in a measured tone, "Sir, more than any of the other pilots here, I was the most skeptical when it came to connecting my mind with that of giant bird to fly missions. I was used to using my hand and gut to control a jet fighter, but after my first test flight, I realized how wrong I was about the program. ROC One responds to my every thought. With ROC One I am able to complete aerial maneuvers at speeds that I never would have thought possible with a jet fighter."

The President smiled. "Thank you, Captain Crow. This country and the rest of the world are putting its faith in you. I can clearly see that our trust is not misplaced."

Crow saluted, and then he began heading toward his quarters.

Captain Green was the next pilot to disengage. She walked with a noticeable limp directly over to the President and saluted him. Then she silently waited for the President to address her.

The President saluted. "Captain Green, what can you tell me about the performance of ROC Three in relation to this mission?"

"ROC Three and I will both give you all that we have, sir."

The President waited for a moment, but he could see that Captain Green was a woman of few words. He dismissed her, and then waited for Captains Munroe and Bixby to disengage from their headsets.

The two young pilots disengaged at almost the same time. They stood from their recliners—smiling and laughing as they excitedly discussed the flights they had taken with the ROCs. They continued to laugh until they noticed that were standing in front of the President.

He smiled at the young pilots. "It seems that you two feel pretty confident about how these ROCs will function against a bunch of giant monsters."

Munroe smiled and tilted her head. "Sir, I can promise you that the ROCs are more than up to the task of taking down these rejects from the History Channel."

The President looked to Bixby, who smiled and looked toward Munroe. "Like she said, sir, we can handle any monster that the Thuggee throw at us."

"Very well, captains, you are dismissed."

The two captains saluted, and then they headed for their quarters.

The President turned to Mackenzie. "Director, I am convinced that the plan you have is our best option. I am going to get on the phone with the leaders of the countries that you have suggested. We are going to have one hell of surprise ready for the Thuggee when their next monster shows up."

CHAPTER 5

The Nest

Bixby grabbed Munroe by her ass, lifted her off of the bed, and slammed her back into the wall. She wrapped her legs around his thighs and her arms around his neck as he continued to drive himself into her. The ROCs had landed at their destinations roughly an hour ago, and after neuro-link, sex had become part of the neuro cool down process for the two pilots.

Munroe screamed as Bixby pushed her closer and closer to climaxing. The two young pilots were not a couple, neither of them was looking for a relationship. They were strictly friends-with-benefits who had both found that after engaging in a neuro-link with the ROCs that they were charged up both physically and mentally.

At first, they tried talking about it as a group, how maybe part of the animal instincts of the creatures' crept into their psyche after the link, but the group therapy sessions did not last long. Crow was the strong silent type, who when presented with an obstacle, simply faced it and dealt with it. Green seemed unwilling or unable to talk about her experience. Both Munroe and Bixby were "actions speak louder than words" types of people, and having sex was one thing that they both excelled at.

Munroe tightened her grip on Bixby and bit down on his ear as she climaxed. She felt him follow suit shortly after her.

When they were done, they would not talk to each other at first. Their ritual would be to get dressed, and then they would go and have a beer and bite to eat while they discussed what their latest flight experience was like. They knew that they did things backward from the way that a couple would do it, with sex before drinks and dinner, but that's why they were friends-with-benefits and not a couple. Sex was one thing, but they each knew they could not develop true romantic feelings for each other. Feelings could compromise a mission and that was one thing that neither of the two of them would let happen.

Bixby was done getting dressed before Munroe, which was fine with him. Watching her pull her clothes over her body was almost as enjoyable as watching her pull them off. Once she was dressed, she turned around and smiled at him. He smiled back at her, and then they left the room together to complete the rest of their sex—beer, food, and talk post ROC ritual.

Green sat in her room with her eyes closed. In her mind, she was replaying the events of her latest flight with ROC 3. Green's right leg had been severely injured when she was shot down on a mission. The medics had been able to save her leg but not by much. She was missing a good deal of muscle, cartilage, and tendons from that leg. Now the leg hurt all of the time, and as a result, her gait was entirely off, which made both her hips and lower back ache all the time as well. She had tried physical therapy, but that process only made her leg hurt more. For a woman who was once a peak level athlete, the pain of barely being able to walk hurt her emotionally far more than it did physically, but that was before ROC 3. Now she knew what it felt like to fly. Not just to fly in a plane but to feel what it physically felt like to have the wind rushing across her face as she soared through the sky. In Green's mind, she knew that her connection with ROC 3 had saved her life. She had been in a deep depression prior to her first neuro-link with the giant bird. Now, when she was sharing a mind with the creature as they flew through the clouds, she was the happiest she had ever been in her entire life.

After a flight, she had a hard time letting go of the experience. She found it best to relive the experience and focus on what she could do the next time that she and ROC 3 were linked together. Once she had her next flight in her mind, she would go to sleep and dream about it. Next to being connected to ROC 3, it was the most enjoyable part of her life.

Crow had his shirt off as he was curling dumbbells and reading article after article about the Jersey Devil, Bigfoot, and the Thuggee off of his tablet. To Crow, all that there was in life was his mission. His current mission consisted of a bunch of creatures that weren't supposed to exist, let alone be giants, and a group of assassin terrorists that were supposed to have been disbanded over a century ago. He knew most of the factions that posed a threat in the world today, but cryptids and ancient cults were two things that he had little knowledge about. Crow was the type of man who believed in the credo of "know your enemy" and that's exactly what he was trying to do now. He heard a soft knock on his door, and by the nature of the knock, he knew exactly who it was. He kept his eyes on his tablet as he said, "Come in, Dr. Curry."

Tracy Curry opened the door to see Crow half naked as sweat poured off of his finely toned body. For brief moment, she forgot why she was there, but a quick look at Crow's computer screen reminded her of the importance of their mission. She walked up to Crow. "How many more times am I going to have to ask you to call me Tracy?"

Crow kept his eyes forward. "At least as many more times as you knock on my door to ask me how I feel about a giant bird when I am trying to exercise and focus on my mission."

Tracy walked in front of Crow so that he was forced to look at her. "Tobias, the other three pilots all have some level of brain wave synchronization with their ROC, but you and ROC One continue to be totally out of sync as far as your thoughts go."

Crow kept exercising as he responded, "The bird does what I tell it to, doesn't it? We have never had any problem with it responding to my commands, have we?"

Tracy shrugged. "That's the problem. You should not feel that you tell ROC One what to do. You should feel that together the two of you accept a course of action based on your knowledge and its instincts."

Crow continued to lift his weights and look at Tracy, with a face that was devoid of emotion. "Dr. Curry, I see that bird the same way that I do a plane, or a rifle, or a knife. It's just a tool that I use to accomplish my mission."

Tracy sighed. "Tobias, ROC One is more than just a bird. It is an intelligent creature whose instincts allowed its kind to survive in an era of Earth's history when the largest and most powerful predators to ever walk the face of the planet were a daily threat. Don't you think that given the current threat we face that learning to tap into those instincts would help you to complete your mission?" She pointed to the tablet behind him. "It would certainly be more helpful than reading about how a hillbilly claims that Bigfoot stole his wife."

Crow didn't respond, so Tracy took a slight step closer to him. "Tobias, the other three pilots all seem to have found ways to deal with their connection to their ROCs. I know that you are a man who keeps his feelings to himself, but in order to get the ROC to function at optimal capacity, you need to let it be a part of you. For that to happen you need to let your thoughts and feelings be open to it." She took a deep breath. "It may help to talk to someone about your experience. If you need someone, I am here for you."

Tracy smiled at Crow, and then she left his quarters as he continued to curl his weights and read about how Bigfoot stole some hillbilly's wife.

The President and director Mackenzie sat in the situation room of Air Force One. The President had just finished calling the countries who were currently housing the ROCs and explaining their role in the crisis the world was facing. The President turned off the feed to the other world leaders and spun around in his chair so that he was facing Mackenzie. "No world leader has responded to Rol-Hama's demands. How much longer do we have until the next attack?"

Mackenzie looked at his watch. "About five hours, sir, but we are ready to confront whatever horror Rol-Hama has prepared next."

The President nodded. "Director, what happens if one of these kaiju kill a ROC when it is still engaged in the neuro-link with the pilot?"

Mackenzie frowned. "All of our projections show that the neuro feedback would overwhelm the pilot's mind. The pilot would survive the experience but their brain would be fried. The pilot would essentially be a vegetable."

CHAPTER 6

Melbourne, Australia

The port was alive with the activity of cargo ships entering and leaving. Dock workers were busy loading and unloading various forms of cargo, from clothing, to automobiles. The cargo ship *Venture* had just pulled into the bay, and it was heading for the dock when it hit something large in the middle of the waterway. The object was large and solid enough that the front end of the *Venture* was crushed upon impact. The captain quickly ordered the ship into full reverse so that they could see what they had hit. As the ship backed up a large swell of water began to form in front of it. A feline-like head with fangs as long as a city bus protruding from it emerged from the water. The creature looked at the *Venture* and roared at the damaged vessel, sending the crew members into a panic.

The creature lifted a massive paw out of the water and brought it crashing down onto the deck of the *Venture*. With a single blow, the kaiju had split the cargo ship in two. The ship's crew members fell into the water where they tried to swim away from the towering creature that stood in front of them. The kaiju roared and smashed its fist into another nearby ship causing it to sink into the bay as well. The kaiju then looked to the city and waded toward the shoreline, revealing a bipedal feline-like creature with long a tail behind it. When a large clawed foot stepped out of the bay and onto shore, the Bunyip stepped out of the realm of myth and folklore, and into the modern world.

The Nest

An alarm blared throughout the Nest, and a voice over the intercom called for Captain Bixby to report to the neuro-link docking station. Bixby had jeans and a t-shirt on as he sprinted through the Nest and ran toward the neuro-link docking area. As he ran into the room with the neuro-link, he saw that Mackenzie was streaming a news feed with Rol-Hama on it. Bixby could hear the fanatic ranting about how it appeared that the leaders of the world had not taken his threats seriously and that the citizens of Melbourne would be the next to feel the wrath of his kaiju.

As Mackenzie heard Bixby running toward him he turned around and stopped the young pilot. "From what we can gather, Rol-Hama has unleashed a kaiju sized version of the cryptid known as the *Bunyip* on Melbourne. The information on the creature is scattered so we don't know much about it. Reports from Melbourne say the monster rose out of the bay and it looks like a giant saber-toothed cat. It's strong enough to smash a freighter with a single blow, and it seems to have the agility of a cat as well. It's moving through the city at a tremendous speed. Get ROC Four into the air and to top speed immediately. Flying at top speed you should be able to engage the kaiju in under twenty minutes. I will have all of the information that we can find on the Bunyip displayed through your neuro-link as you are in flight."

Bixby nodded, jumped into his recliner, and pulled his neuro-link helmet over his head as adrenaline rushed through his system. As he was linking with ROC 4, the thought crossed his mind that sex with Munroe was awesome after taking ROC 4 on test flights, and he wondered what it would be like after engaging in an active battle. Bixby's thoughts were quickly focused on the mission as his view was replaced by the scenery around ROC 4. Bixby whispered, "All right, boy, let's go kick some cryptid ass!" A moment later ROC 4 was soaring through the air toward Melbourne .

Bixby was about five minutes into his flight when the information on the Bunyip appeared in front of him through his neuro-link:

Bunyip – A monster reported to live in bodies of water located throughout Australia. The creature's names means "water spirit."

Descriptions – Descriptions of the creature vary wildly including a dog-like face or crocodile head, dark shaggy fur, flippers and walrus tusks. The creature is reported to come out of water holes and attack people that it sees as a threat to it or its habitat.

Current data from attack – The creature is bipedal, covered in fur, and has long tusks. It stands over 280 feet tall and weighs in excess of 5,000 tons.

Melbourne

The buildings near the bay were already reduced to smoking ruins. The local police and emergency response teams were working to evacuate the city as quickly as possible. They knew that trying to engage the kaiju directly would only cost them more lives. The government had assured the police that help was on the way and that they could assist by helping to get as many civilians out of the way as possible.

The Bunyip was approaching a large building, and he was lifting his claw above his head to tear into it when he heard a strange sound coming from the sky above him. The Bunyip looked up to see the majestic form of ROC 4 soaring above him.

ROC 4 flew past the Bunyip once so that Bixby could gauge for himself exactly what he was facing. ROC 4 circled around and dove directly at the Bunyip, dropping a dozen of its diamond coated metal feathers onto the cryptid. The large blades dug into the Bunyip's body. ROC 4 streaked up into the air, and through its eyes, Bixby saw the long blades sticking out of the monster's arms, shoulders, chest, and thighs. The cryptid was clearly in pain from the attack, but the blades didn't seem to cause much damage to the creature. The Bunyip was quickly pulling the painful feathers from his body as Bixby had ROC 4 circle back around for another attack.

ROC 4 dove at the Bunyip. When ROC 4 reached the cryptid it viscously attacked the monster using its beak and claws to rake the Bunyip's head and face. The Bunyip attempted in vain to claw and bite at ROC 4 before he backhanded the cybernetic kaiju and sent it crashing into a nearby building. Through his neuro-link, Bixby felt that the blow had stunned ROC 4. Bixby was urging ROC 4 to pull itself out of the collapsed section of the building while the Bunyip drew ever closer.

ROC 4 was just starting to get to its feet when the Bunyip brought its fist crashing into ROC 4's face. The blow sent ROC 4's head slamming into the remains of the building. The blow was flowed by a kick to ROC 4's midsection that drove the giant bird farther into the remains of the structure. The Bunyip roared at his downed opponent, and then he slashed at ROC 4 with his long claws.

Watching through ROC 4's eyes Bixby instinctively threw his arms up in front of him to shield his face. His motion caused ROC 4 to move its diamond coated metal feathered wings in front of its face. The Bunyip's claws sent sparks flying into the sky as they scratched harmlessly across the diamond coated feathers. Bixby didn't waste a second, he urged ROC 4 to spring forward and unload his freezing liquid nitrogen spray into the face of the Bunyip. The spray covered the Bunyip's face and torso.

The kaiju roared in pain as he felt his eyes, fangs, tongue and fur freezing.

With the Bunyip stunned, ROC 4 pulled itself out of the skeletal remains of the building. Bixby immediately sent the cyborg into the air. ROC 4 circled its prey a couple of times and Bixby could feel exactly how the instincts inside of the bird wanted to attack the Bunyip. Bixby trusted ROC 4 and directed it to proceed with its planned method of attack. ROC 4 screeched and then circled behind the Bunyip before slamming into the cryptid and knocking him to the ground face first.

ROC 4 quickly landed on the Bunyip's back and dug its claws into the monster's shoulders. Before the Bunyip could react to the attack, ROC 4 bent down with its beak and began savagely tearing into the back of the Bunyip's neck. Within seconds, ROC 4 had clamped its beak around the Bunyip's spinal cord. ROC 4 focused on tearing the spinal cord to pieces as the Bunyip tried in vain to lift his body off of the ground. After several seconds of attacking the Bunyip' spinal cord, ROC 4 had succeeded in tearing it to pieces. The Bunyip roared in defiance as his now paralyzed body laid useless on the street. ROC 4 screeched and then began tearing into the defenseless Bunyip's face until the beast finally perished.

Back in the Nest, Bixby could hear a cheer of joy echo throughout the neuro-link room. Bixby smiled as he realized that he and ROC 4 had won the first battle of this war. He had directed ROC 4 to return to his waiting station where it could be fed and its weapons systems reloaded.

ROC 4 was in the air and Bixby was removing his neuro-link helmet when he heard the alarm blare throughout the Nest again.

Bixby got his helmet off and looked to his right to see Munroe jumping into her recliner and putting on her neuro-link helmet.

CHAPTER 7

Democratic Republic of the Congo, Kinshasa

The people of the city of Kinshasa were not surprised to see a creature resembling a sauropod dinosaur that the modern world did not believe existed swimming down the Congo River and approaching their city. Many of their ancestors had spoken of the Mokele-Mbembe and the natives in the jungle still occasionally saw the creature. Two things surprised the people of Kinshasa, first, the creature's size. The Mokele-Mbembe was known to be large, larger than even the mighty elephant, but the creature that they now beheld dwarfed even their largest buildings. The name Mokele-Mbembe meant "He whose body stops the flow of rivers." The creature's body was so large that it almost looked like it could block the ocean from changing tides.

The second thing that surprised the people of Kinshasa was that the monster had swum far enough down the river that it was approaching the city. For centuries, the monster had remained in the most isolated parts of the Congo River, deep in the heart of the jungle. To see the kaiju wading toward the city elicited feelings of both fear and curiosity.

While some people were fleeing away from the river, others were walking toward it to see the creature that they had heard their grandparents and great-grandparents speak of with such respect. The Mokele-Mbembe stepped out of the river and onto the streets of Kinshasa. The beast bellowed once, lifted his foot off of the ground, and then brought it crashing back down. The kaiju's foot hit the street with such force that it created a powerful shockwave. The shockwave hit the surrounding streets and buildings as if it were a centralized earthquake. The street in front of the Mokele-Mbembe split in two, and the four buildings closest to the monster crumbled to dust under the force of the shockwave. The windows of the buildings in a five block radius shattered, raining down shards of glass onto the people walking below them. The Mokele-Mbembe bellowed once again and started walking farther into the city spreading death and destruction with each step the cryptid took.

Munroe had ROC 2 in the air almost as soon as the alarm had gone off. She was near the neuro-link watching as Bixby engaged the monster in Australia, and as soon as she saw the word *Africa* go across the bottom of the TV screen, she jumped into her chair. ROC 2 was in the air and moving at top speed as soon as possible, but from the updates that she was receiving, ROC 2's top speed may not be fast enough. The Mokele-Mbembe was literally crushing Kinshasa into rubble.

Mackenzie was feeding her real-time updates both verbally and through the display on her neuro-link. There seemed to be no need to worry about civilian casualties when she engaged the monster. From reports in the city, it seemed that everyone within a five block radius of the monster was dying almost instantly as a result of the powerful shockwaves that Mokele-Mbembe was giving off as he walked.

While she was in mid-flight, Mackenzie had compiled everything that he could on the Mokele-Mbembe:

Mokele-Mbembe – a Cryptid reported to live in the Congo River Basin. Its name means "One Whose Body stops the flow of rivers."

Descriptions – The creature is said to be a large sauropod like dinosaur with a long neck, a thin powerful body, and a long tail. The creature is said to be very territorial and extremely powerful. There are several reports where people have claimed to see the creature slay the likes of crocodiles, hippopotamus, and even elephants that had entered its territory.

Current data from attack – The creature is quadruped and it is extremely large . It is roughly 600 feet in length and over 500 feet tall at the top of its head. It weighs in excess of 20,000 tones

Thirty minutes after she had taken flight, Munroe could see the devastated remains of Kinshasa through ROC 2's eyes. The bird's eyes perceived not only unimaginable destruction, but a death toll in the millions, as countless bodies could be seen sprawled across what was left of the city's streets. Munroe realized that even her best efforts had not been enough to save those people, but she promised them that she would end the Mokele-Mbembe here and now in order to prevent the creature from recreating this horror in another city.

The information that she had received on the Mokele-Mbembe was extremely accurate. The kaiju was so large that Munroe was able to spot the creature instantly. The kaiju looked like the pictures of the Apatosaurus that she had seen in dinosaur books as a kid, except that this creature was far larger than any dinosaur that had ever existed. ROC 2 was over two hundred and fifty feet from beak to tail feathers, and the Mokele-Mbembe was easily three times that length. Munroe figured that the monster must have weighed easily ten times as much as ROC 2. The cryptid reminded Munroe of the stories of the legendary Leviathan from the Bible. The Mokele-Mbembe was truly a kaiju amongst kaiju.

Munroe had ROC 2 fly low over the monster, and like Bixby, she began her attack by dropping a barrage of diamond coated feather blades onto the creature. ROC 2 flew the length of the creature's body leaving a trail of feather blades from its tail to its head. If the Mokele-Mbembe felt the attack he didn't show it. The beast simply kept walking forward toward what little was left of the city of Kinshasa. Munroe was sure that almost all of the survivors from the attack would currently be huddled in the remains of the city, and she was determined to save them.

She had ROC 2 fly to a spot three hundred feet directly in front of the Mokele-Mbembe, and then she hovered at eye level with the behemoth. ROC 2 began to flap its wings at a rapid pace causing hurricane force winds to strike the Mokele-Mbembe. In addition to the wall of wind, chunks of debris and abandoned vehicles were lifted off the ground and slammed into the Mokele-Mbembe. Despite that attack, the powerful creature continued to walk forward as if he were encountering nothing more than a cool breeze kicking up some dead leaves. Seeing that her attack was having no effect, Munroe recalled Bixby's battle and attempted to utilize the same strategy. ROC 2 suddenly streaked toward the Mokele-Mbembe with the intention of latching onto the cryptid's neck and attacking its spinal column. With a speed that defied its size, the Mokele-Mbembe's head dipped down, and then shot up crashing into ROC 2, sending the mighty cyborg tumbling through the air.

ROC 2 crashed to the ground and skidded into the rubble of what was once the business district of Kinshasa. ROC 2 was beginning to stand when the long, thick tail of the Mokele-Mbembe smashed into its side and sent the cyborg's body rolling over countless tons of ragged debris. Munroe sensed that ROC 2 could not take much more of this punishment. There was no way that even the mighty bird could stand toe to toe with the behemoth and hope to survive. The Mokele-Mbembe was simply too powerful for ROC 2 to engage head-on. She needed to get ROC 2 into the air, and then use its speed and her cunning to defeat this juggernaut. ROC 2 was lying flat on its stomach when the colossal jaws of the Mokele-Mbembe clamped down on its left wing and lifted the cyborg into the air. The pressure was immense, and Munroe knew that if it were not for the diamond coated feathers on ROC 2's wing that the appendage would have been crushed as if it were cardboard. With the thought of the feathers in her mind, Munroe directed ROC 2 to fire several of the feathers on its left wing into the mouth of the Mokele-Mbembe. Dozens of blades suddenly sliced into the soft tissue of the sauropod's mouth, causing it to bleed profusely, and forcing him to release ROC 2.

The Mokele-Mbembe shook his head from side to side in an attempt to free the blades from his mouth. ROC 2 circled the cryptid twice as Munroe considered how best to use her speed advantage over the monster. ROC 2 dived toward the Mokele-Mbembe, and Munroe directed it to fly in a tight circle around the cryptid's head. ROC 2 circled the giant's head once, and then it turned its beak toward the Mokele-Mbembe's face and started spraying it with liquid nitrogen. ROC 2 continued to circle the kaiju's head and spray it with liquid nitrogen until both tanks within its neck were completely empty. ROC 2 pulled off for a second so that Munroe could get a good look at the monster. It looked like the Mokele-Mbembe's head was frozen solid, but Munroe was not taking any chances. ROC 2 dove at the Mokele-Mbembe's head with its claws out in front of it. ROC 2 smashed through the frozen head like it was a piñata—causing frozen pieces of skull and brain to fall down on the remains of the city. The headless body of the Mokele-Mbembe shuddered for moment, and then it fell to its side causing one last earthquake when it hit ground.

ROC 2 flew one victorious circle over the corpse of the monster before heading back to Morocco. With ROC 2's flight pattern in the bird's mind, Munroe pulled the neuro-link helmet off of her head, and screamed, "Whoooo! That takes care of two of those bastards!" She jumped up and hugged Bixby, who was standing next to her recliner. The two of them were debriefed by Mackenzie, and then they dashed back to Bixby's room. Several hours later Bixby's room looked as if the Mokele-Mbembe had walked past it—furniture and clothing had been tossed all over the place.

CHAPTER 8

Tribal Region of Pakistan

Hundreds of the Thuggee cultists gathered before the court of Rol-Hama as he passed judgement on his followers, who had been tasked with unleashing both the Bunyip and the Mokele-Mbembe onto the world. The two cultists who had sent the monstrous cryptids to attack the cities of Melbourne and Kinshasa were kneeling in front of Rol-Hama and staring out at their fellow cult members from a small stage. Both men were dressed in their full ceremonial garb with bright red turbans wrapped tightly around their heads and long white robes draped over their bodies. Behind the stage, loomed the massive statue of Kali herself.

Rol-Hama wore a headdress that was patterned after the goddess Kali. He wore no shirt, and only a pair of khakis that strained to maintain their consistency against Rol-Hama's muscular thighs. The leader of the Thuggee was as intelligent as he was insane. He purposely took advantage of every situation that he could to show off his hulking body to his followers. He knew full well that his physically intimidating appearance only helped to strengthen the psychological fear that his followers already felt toward their leader. Rol-Hama walked behind the two men who under his command had dispatched the two kaiju to their respective targets.

Rol-Hama paced back and forth behind the two men, with a long scimitar in his hand. He stopped between the two men and held the scimitar over his head so that what little light was in the room glinted off of the weapon. Rol-Hama addressed his followers, "The two men that you see before you are guilty! Guilty of the most heinous crime that can be committed in the eyes of all powerful Kali!"

Rol-Hama looked over his gathered followers to see that each of them had their eyes fixed on him. The madman silently hoped that he would find a pair of them whispering to each other, or even a single man who was simply staring off into space, so that he could make an example of them as well. To his dismay, Rol-Hama was unable to find a follower who was not hanging on his every word. He pushed the thought from his mind. The next time that he held a meeting he could falsely accuse someone of having a wandering mind, and then make an example of him. For today, he had his two examples, and he continued his speech in regards to their crime, "These two men are guilty of the crime of failure! They have failed Kali herself by sending out the creatures which Kali has given to us as her avatars here on Earth. They have failed in the service of Kali, and the punishment is . . . death!"

Rol-Hama placed his hand on the shoulder of the first man, and then he placed the point of his scimitar against the man's back. Rather than quickly ending the man's life, Rol-Hama stood behind him for a minute. Once more he did this for dramatic effect. The man in front of him would have a brave visage for a moment or two, but with each passing second longer that he had to ponder his death, more fear would creep onto his face. The gathered cultists who were watching the proceeding would see this fear and remember it. More importantly, they would remember that it was Rol-Hama that had inspired this fear. When Rol-Hama could see the sweat pouring down the man's face, he finally drove the sword into the man's back and through his chest. The Thuggee leader was careful to miss the man's heart and only to cut his lung.

The man screamed in pain as Rol-Hama slowly pulled out the hooked sword, once more slicing into the man's lung. By missing the heart and puncturing the lung, Rol-Hama had ensured the man a slow and painful death. The man fell to the floor and moaned in pain as he grabbed the gaping wound in his chest and slowly drowned to death in his own blood.

Rol-Hama placed his hand on the shoulder of the second man. He kept his hand on the second man's shoulder and waited for the first man to slowly expire. Rol-Hama wanted the man to be fully aware of the painful death that was ahead of him, and more importantly, he wanted the rest of his followers to see the mental torture that he put the second man through. Once the first man had stopped writhing on the floor, Rol-Hama drove his sword into the back of the second man, and once more he made sure to miss the heart and puncture the lung.

Rol-Hama stood silently above the dying man until the last spark of life seeped out of his body. Once the man had perished, Rol-Hama first turned and held the bloody sword up in front of the statue of Kali. He then addressed the rest of his followers, "The enemies of Kali have their own monsters in the form of giant birds. Clearly these birds are the avatars of the Garuda. The bird-beast who is the servant of Vishnu. The sworn enemy of Kali and of the Thuggee. These men were unprepared to face the children of Garuda. Do not let yourselves be caught unaware. Be prepared to face Vishnu, Garuda, and the enemies of Kali in whatever form they may take. Go and prepare yourselves, for in twelve hours, we shall strike again, and this time we shall slay the children of Garuda. Praise Kali!"

A chant of "Praise Kali" ran through the crowd.

After the gathered cultists had dispersed, Rol-Hama climbed down the back of the stage and walked through a hidden door behind the statue of Kali. Rol-Hama had entered a private cell room that, unbeknownst to most his followers, held a secret prison. Two scared and emaciated men sat in two separate cells. The two men each looked as if they had not been bathed, shaved, had a change of clothes, or been offered much to eat in weeks. Their cells had a rough cot with a bug ridden mattress and a simple bowl to use as a toilet. Rats, mice, and cockroaches could be seen scurrying in and out of the cells, grabbing the few crumbs that had fallen on the floor. The only comfort that the two cells had was a video screen next to it with a live feed to a different house. Currently, both screens were alternating scenes of a woman and two to three children sleeping soundly in their beds.

Rol-Hama stared at the two screens for a moment, and then he smiled at them. He then began addressing the two captives, "Ah, gentlemen, for two people who are not believers in all powerful Kali you have been blessed with beautiful families." The cultist watched the video feeds for a brief moment before smiling at the two men. "It seems that both of your families are getting on well with their lives after we led them to believe that you had both perished in automobile accidents." He pointed to video feeds. "As you can see, I have kept my word. As long as you continue to provide me with the knowledge I need to properly utilize the monsters, your families will be spared."

The man in the cell to the right of Rol-Hama sat up on his bed. "Those creatures are just wild beasts that you had me install behavior modification chips into their brains so that they would follow your basic commands. They have lived peacefully for thousands of years. You're the one who is threatening to murder our families if we don't do what you say. As far as I can tell, you are the only monster here."

Rol-Hama laughed. "My dear Dr. Tieg, I would never threaten the lives of women and children. Why would I have them killed when their lives could be spent in service to me?" He quickly looked to the other cell. "You, and doctor Branson, have done surprisingly well for yourselves in finding a mate. I commend the two of you. You both have beautiful wives. Beautiful wives who could each serve me as fine concubines if I so desired them to."

Dr. Tieg sprang at the door to his cage. "You bastard! If you so much as lay hand on my wife I'll kill you!"

Rol-Hama laughed again. "I think not, Dr. Teig, and know that the fate of your wives will be paradise at my side compared to what will happen to your children should you disobey me or should the creatures fail to carry out my plan." Rol-Hama glared into the eyes of Dr. Teig. "I may not have the knowledge to alter thoughts and behaviors through surgeries and implants, but rest assured, I do know how to alter behaviors through reward and punishment." Rol-Hama smiled. "Look at my followers and see how well my methods work on grown men. Just imagine what a strict program of punishment for thinking freely and rewards for obeying my commands could do for the young impressionable minds of your children."

Dr. Teig slowly backed away from the bars of his cell and sat down on his cot. Rol-Hama nodded at him, and then he walked over to the keyboard that was linked to the two screens. He stopped the feed of the men's families and brought up videos of the battles between the ROCs and the Bunyip and the Mokele-Mbembe. The cult leader then folded his legs and sat down on the floor in between the two cells. "Gentlemen, I would ask you to watch the videos of these two encounters, and then we shall discuss how the implications of these events shall affect my plans going forward."

The two scientists watched the videos in silence, and after they had concluded, Rol-Hama spoke, "To win a war a man must know his enemies, and currently, I know very little about these *ROCs*, as the news reporters are referring to them as. Let me tell what I do know. I know that while these ROCs have obvious cybernetic components to them, they are still clearly giant animals. I also know that birds do not grow to the size that these creatures have attained without some outside influence. From watching the videos of these creatures, I can also tell that the ROCs are controlled by a human intelligence. No mere animal changes its battle tactics as quickly as those creatures did based on their enemies attributes and attack patterns. This also tells me that whoever is controlling these creatures has a much greater degree of influence than we currently have over our kaiju."

Rol-Hama paused for a second and stared at the two men before continuing. "Gentlemen, I do not know much about this enemy, but given that each of you are the top researchers and professors in your fields, I would suggest that each of you know a great deal about these ROCs and the people who are behind them."

He first looked to Dr. Branson's cell. "Dr. Branson, it was you who provided me with the growth serum that helped our cryptids attain such massive heights. It was that same formula that also helped increase the density of our creatures' skin and muscles making them virtually indestructible. Given the size of these ROCs, would you think that they underwent a similar process as our cryptids?"

The doctor stammered, "I...I ..I would think so, yes."

Rol-Hama nodded. "Good. Now, Dr. Teig, please explain to me how the people behind these ROCs are able to control these creatures to a level that is so far beyond the influence that we have our cryptids."

Teig shrugged. "The chips that I implanted in the cryptid's brains allows you to send images directly into their minds. So far you have basically sent the cryptids pictures of things like a city, people, and then death and destruction. The implants in their brains act to have the creatures believe that these images are their desires, and the creatures act on those desires. You show Bigfoot a picture of San Jose in ruins, he thinks that the he should destroy San Jose, and then he attacks the city." Teig sighed. "These ROCs seem to have some kind of direct neuro-link with a controller who can influence their every movement. Comparing the two processes is like comparing the job of a butcher in a deli to a skilled surgeon."

Rol-Hama smiled. "You see? I knew the two of you must have had some idea about these ROCs. Now comes the more difficult part of our discussion. The two of you are the only specialists in the world who were working on enlarging creatures to the size of giants and using implants to control thought processes. As I said, you are both also top the professors in your fields. This leads me to suspect that the people who created these ROCs and the system that is used to control them were at one time students of yours. Students who at this point may have even surpassed your brilliance and accomplishments. This would mean that these students would have been some of your best and brightest minds."

Rol-Hama stood. "Now gentlemen, I want you to spend the next twenty-four hours compiling a list of former students of yours that you think could have accomplished these goals. You will present me with this list tomorrow, and I shall use other information at my disposal to determine which of these former students are behind the creation of these ROCs. Once I have that information, I will be able to apply pressure to these individuals to provide the means of rendering these ROCs inert." The madman smiled. "Now gentlemen, I can see from the looks on your faces that supplying me with list of your former students does not sit well with you, but I would suggest you weigh the well-being of your students against the well-being of your families. I am sure that once you consider the potential futures for your families that I detailed earlier that you will be able to construct these lists with a clear conscious. If you will excuse me now, I have only ten hours until I began the next round of attacks."

Rol-Hama turned and walked out of his hidden dungeon as Dr. Branson and Dr. Teig sat in stunned silence.

Chapter 9

The sun shined on ROC 3, and the wind blew across its massive wings as it continued to fly in a large circle around parts of China, Russia, India, and Pakistan. The clock was ticking, and Rol-Hama's next round of attacks were due to start at any second. Rather than wait for the threat to originate, Green had ROC 3 already in the air and circling the part of the world under her protection. Aside from having ROC 3 ready to respond to a threat, it also gave Green the excuse to spend more time neuro-linked with ROC 3. When she was linked to ROC 3 she felt as if she had left her now deficient body and had joined with the body of a god. A god with a body that was powerful beyond imagination. A god that was uninhibited by the constraints of her body. A god that could fly, and when she and ROC 3 were soaring through the air, it was the only time that Green felt truly alive.

Her mind and that of ROC 3 were perfectly synced together. Each thought that Green had blended seamlessly with the natural movements, reactions, and instincts of ROC 3. Green's peaceful flight with ROC 3 was abruptly cut short as an alarm sounded throughout the Nest and information suddenly appeared in her view of the sky through ROC 3's eyes. In big green letters, she read the words:

New Delhi, India, under attack. Proceed to New Delhi and engage target. More information to follow.

The moment that Green had dreaded had finally arrived. Green was a veteran of dozens of combat missions. The fear that she felt was not of the coming battle itself but of the danger presented to ROC 3. She had flown dozens of planes and jets throughout her career, but they were just machines, soulless constructs that she had used to accomplish a mission. ROC 3 was different from any vehicle that she had ever flown. ROC 3 was a living, breathing creature with a soul. A creature that had given her a purpose in life, a reason to continue living, a way in which she could still experience the world, and now its life would be put in danger.

ROC 3 could sense the distress in Green's mind, and while the kaiju could not communicate in any method recognizable to humans, Green was able to understand the bird's desires. She could sense that ROC 3 was hungry for battle. Green was also fully aware that ROC 3's desire was largely due to her thought process. Like any soldier, Green saw the area that she was assigned to as her duty to protect. Those same thoughts when processed through ROC 3's mind became a desire to defend what the kaiju perceived as its territory. Green whispered to herself, "All right then, let's do this." She directed ROC 3 to veer south toward New Delhi and to increase to its top speed as the information on her target appeared in her field of vision:

Monkey Man – A strange monkey-like creature who appeared in New Delhi in 2001 where it attacked and killed dozens of people over the course of several months.

Descriptions – The creature is said to have a thin monkey-like body with long claws and a human-like face.

Current data from attack – The creature is bipedal, stands roughly 250 feet tall. It is tall and thin weighing roughly 2,000 tons. The creature is reported to be an excellent jumper.

New Delhi, India

Ashan Carr rushed his young daughter through the crowded streets of New Delhi as the horror behind them continued to reach a frenzied pitch. He looked briefly over his shoulder to see a mob of people running and screaming in terror. The strange thing was that Ashan could no longer see what the mob was running from. As Ashan was looking back, the sun suddenly disappeared from above him. Ashan, his daughter, and everyone around them were suddenly shrouded in darkness.

Ashan looked up, and his vision was filled with a streak of dark black fur soaring overhead. A second later a dark shape came crashing down on the people in the front of the fleeing mob. Ashan beheld a long, slender, hair covered body crouched before him. The creature was huge. Even in its crouched position its horrible face was higher than the four story buildings next to it. The face appeared simian in nature but with a faint trace of humanity in it. Behind the face, a long and thin tail twitched back and forth in the air. The monster had the build of a monkey but with the long powerful torso of a man. The creature looked like the god Hanuman had come to Earth. A decade prior, a smaller version of the creature had been seen in the city, and the media had dubbed the beast Monkey Man.

Ashan screamed in horror as the now giant Monkey Man stood before him. This was the second time that Ahsan had encountered the Monkey Man. He had first encountered the creature when he was a boy and the beast was terrorizing the city. Back then, the monster was only about six feet tall. Ashan did not know how the beast had grown so large, but he knew that it made an already vicious creature even more deadly than it had been in its previous incarnation. Ashan saw the kaiju lift its paw up next its head, and he knew what would happen next. The mob turned to run in the opposite direction, but Ashan pushed his daughter to the ground and then threw himself on top of her. Ashan felt a something huge brush across his back as he kept his daughter pressed to the ground beneath him.

He moved his head from side to side as he scanned the now empty street. He rolled on his back, and to his horror, he saw the paw of Monkey Man stuffing a handful of screaming people into his mouth. The mob running from the beast a second ago was now being torn to pieces by the monster's saber-like teeth. Ashan kept his daughter pressed beneath his body as he stared at the horror above him. When he had faced the Monkey Man as a boy, Ashan had prayed to Vishnu to protect him from the monster. On that day, his prayers were answered as several police officers appeared and chased the Monkey Man away.

With no other option left for him, Ashan prayed to Vishnu again. This time he was not praying for himself but for the life of his daughter. To his astonishment, Ashan's prayers were answered once again. There was loud screech behind him, and less than a second later, he saw a gigantic feathered creature streaking down from the sky.

The giant bird grabbed the Monkey Man's tail and then it dragged the cryptid down the street and away from Ashan and his daughter. Ashan stood up and picked up his daughter. "Look, my love, our prayers have been answered! Vishnu has sent the Garuda to protect us from the demon. Remember this miracle and praise Vishnu for all the days of your life."

ROC 3 continued to drag the Monkey Man down through the streets of New Delhi. Green had turned on the infrared function in

ROC 3's eyes, and she was using it to make sure that she was dragging the monster through a path that had the least amount of people as possible. She was hoping that ROC 3 would be able to drag the Monkey Man clear of the city before engaging him in battle, but that hope was extinguished when the Monkey Man dug his claws into the asphalt and brought himself and ROC 3 to a dead stop. ROC 3 couldn't react fast enough to drop the Monkey Man's tail, which caused the tail to stretch and then snap back bringing ROC 3 crashing into the back of the man-beast.

ROC 3 stood and turned around to see the Monkey Man leaping at it. The two kaiju were a blur of teeth, claws, feathers, and beak as they tried to tear each other to pieces. Blood was flying from both creatures and covering the nearby buildings in crimson. Green knew that if the battle persisted in this manner that ROC 3 would not last very long. At Green's suggestion, ROC 3 opened its beak and sprayed the Monkey Man with liquid nitrogen.

The nimble creature leapt backward. His fur was covered in frost, but otherwise, the kaiju was unharmed by the attack. The Monkey Man flipped into the air and cleared an entire street of buildings. He landed on the parallel street, and then he crouched down low so that the buildings shielded him from his opponent.

ROC 3 began flapping its wings as it tried to get back into the air. The winged kaiju had taken to the sky and had reached an altitude of several hundred feet when it spotted the Monkey Man on the street below it. ROC 3 was swooping in to drop its feather blades on the beast when the Monkey Man sprung into the air and grabbed ROC 3 by the neck. ROC 3's flight pattern was disrupted and the two monsters came crashing back to Earth—with ROC 3 taking the worst of the impact.

The Monkey Man jumped on top of ROC 3, and then the savaged creature began biting and clawing at the massive bird. ROC 3's torso was being ripped to shreds by the cryptid as feathers, skin, and blood flew into the air and became matted in the hair of the grotesque Monkey Man.

ROC 3 spread its wings out and began to fire its feather-like blades at the man-beast. The Monkey Man screeched in pain as the feather blades embedded themselves into the kaiju's sides. Once more the Monkey Man tumbled backward to avoid the attack.

ROC 3 stood and took to the air as quickly as possible. It flew one tight circle, and then crashed into the Monkey Man, knocking the primate onto its back. ROC 3 flew a circle around the Monkey Man and once again it started to fire its feather blades at the monster.

The Monkey Man ignored the searing pain that each feather inflicted on it, and despite the relentless attack, the Monkey Man forced his body into a crouching position. With his feet below him, the man-beast once more leapt at ROC 3 in an attempt to knock the avian kaiju from the sky.

Green and ROC 3 were ready for the monster's attack. As soon as ROC 3 saw the Monkey Man crouching down, Green had it alter its flight pattern. The cryptid missed the cyborg, and it landed back in the city streets. ROC 3 flew behind the Monkey Man as the cryptid was trying to regain his balance from his missed leap as ROC 3 began to flap its wings and hover in place.

The flapping of ROC 3's wings caused a powerful wind shear to slam into the Monkey Man's back. The monster stumbled forward and fell face first into an apartment complex. ROC 3 flew to the fallen Monkey Man and dug its talons into the Monkey Man's shoulders. The beast screeched in pain as ROC 3's talons tore through skin and muscles before burying themselves in bone. ROC 3 looked to the sky, and then it began to flap its wings. The people of New Delhi watched in awe as ROC 3 lifted the slender Monkey Man off the ground and took off into the sky with the horrid beast.

The Monkey Man shook its body and attempted to slash at ROC 3 but even his long arms were unable to reach the colossal raptor. ROC 3 continued to soar higher into the air and away from the city. ROC 3 increased its speed, and within five minutes, it had exited the city and was over the countryside with the Monkey Man still struggling helplessly below it. With civilians and collateral damage no longer a concern, Green let ROC 3's instincts take over. Between the long flight and the battle, ROC 3 had expended a good deal of energy, and now the beast was hungry.

ROC 3 looked down at the flailing Monkey Man and the cyborg's perception of the monster quickly changed from enemy to food. ROC 3's beak shot down and tore out the Monkey Man's right eye, and then swallowed it whole. The Monkey Man's left eye quickly suffered the same fate. The blinded creature wailed in pain and terror as ROC 3 used its beak to strike at the cryptid's skull. After a dozen painful strikes to the head, the Monkey Man's skull finally split open and allowed ROC 3 access to the cryptid's brain. ROC 3 tore out a huge chunk of grey matter, and finally, the Monkey Man stopped his pitiful struggle.

ROC 3 dropped the giant corpse into an open field where it crashed into the ground and created a large crater. ROC 3 circled the corpse several times before landing and gorging itself on the remains of the monster. ROC 3 fed for nearly an hour on its defeated foe, and in that time an army of buzzards had begun to circle overhead waiting for ROC 3 to finish its grizzly meal so that they could partake of the leftovers. Throughout the entire process, Green did not disengage from ROC 3. She felt that she and ROC 3 were one and the same creature, and she wanted to experience each and every aspect of ROC 3's life. When ROC 3 finished eating, it looked to the sky at the hundreds of buzzards waiting for their master to finish his meal.

Green had compared having a neuro-link with ROC 3 to being akin to sharing one's existence with a god. As Green saw the buzzards circling overhead and cackling in joy at the feast ROC 3 had brought them, she realized that to these creatures ROC 3 was a god, and so was she. To a woman who mere months ago viewed herself as a cripple, the idea of herself as a god was intoxicating. In her mind, Sheena Green was ROC 3, and ROC 3 was Sheena Green. Together the two of them were the rulers of the sky and all of its inhabitants. ROC 3 screeched, and in her recliner back in the Nest, Green did the same. ROC 3 then took to the air and began flying back to its resting spot in Russia.

The other pilots, as well as Mackenzie and Tracy Curry, were all standing near Green watching her battle with the Monkey Man through the video feed.

Tracy was splitting her attention between the video feed and the display showing the neuro-link between ROC 3 and Green. Green and ROC 3 had always had the most powerful link of any of the pilots and the ROCs. Tracy was able to determine this by watching two waves on a screen representing the pilot and the ROCs brainwaves. Green and ROC 3's brainwaves were often extremely close and occasionally they even overlapped, indicating a very strong neuro-link.

When Green let loose her scream, Tracy's eyes went wide as she watched the two lines representing the brainwaves of Green and ROC 3 merge into a single wave.

CHAPTER 10

Tracy knew what the single wavelength meant. Instead of two coexisting thought processes, there was one single stream of consciousness. Captain Green was losing herself in ROC 3. Tracy grabbed her microphone, and spoke in a calm voice, "Captain Green, we need you to break your connection with ROC Three so that we can evaluate the condition of both of you after the battle."

Green didn't move. "I'm fine."

Tracy sighed. "Okay, Captain Green, but ROC 3 suffered a good amount of damage in the battle. In order to fully assess how badly it was hurt, we need you to break your link with ROC 3."

Green screamed, "I'm fine!"

The fact that Green had used the word *I* when she was referring to ROC 3 scared her. Captain Crow was standing next to her, and she looked at him, with pleading eyes. "Tobias, I need to disconnect Captain Green from ROC Three. I am not sure that she is in control of herself right now."

Tobias nodded, and he followed Tracy as she approached Green.

Tracy was concerned that Green would react negatively to the two of them approaching her, but she was so engrossed in ROC 3, that she appeared to be totally unaware of what was going on around her physical body. Tracy motioned to Crow that she was going to pull Green's helmet off and that he needed to be ready to grab Green. Crow nodded that he understood her command. Tracy grabbed Green's neuro-link helmet and pulled it off of her head.

The moment that the helmet came off, Green screamed, and her body began to convulse as if she was having a seizure.

Crow held onto to her to make sure that she did not fall off of her recliner and hurt herself. Sixty seconds had passed before Green regained control of her body. Crow was still holding her as she burst into tears.

Tracy walked over to her. "Captain Green, I think that you should—"

Green screamed, "NOOOO! NO, you don't get to think about what I should do! They already took my leg from me. I won't let you take my wings! Do you know what's it's like to have every step you take hurt? To see crutches and a wheelchair in your future? This is what I felt, and then you gave me the ability to fly. To fly through the air like a god!"

Tracy tried to place her hand on Green's shoulder, but the pilot shrugged it off. Tracy knelt and looked Green in the eye. "Some of these thoughts are yours, but the experiences you are talking about belong to ROC Three. The anguish over your leg is yours, but the feeling of flight belongs to ROC Three. You have to think of your neuro-link with ROC Three like you would a relationship with a person. It's good to be close to each other, to understand each other, to want to be together, but for the relationship to grow you each have to be individuals. You need to grow separately as individuals so that when you are together the two of you are greater than the sum of individual parts."

Green cried, "You don't understand. I can fly."

Tracy turned away from Green. "I am taking you off of active duty until I have time to complete a psychological evaluation on you and your neuro-link with ROC Three has the chance to fade a little bit."

Green grabbed Tracy's hand. "Please, Dr. Curry, you can't take my wings away from me. You can't!"

Tracy shook her head. "They're not *your* wings. They are ROC Three's wings, and that's exactly why I need to you off of active duty."

Green started cursing at Tracy as Crow lifted her up and helped her to her quarters. Green sobbed as Crow supported her. "She doesn't understand. She doesn't understand."

Crow maintained his silence as she continued to sob. He helped her to bed, closed the door, and walked back to Tracy.

Bixby and Munroe quietly slipped out of the room to grab a quick drink after the drama they had just witnessed.

Tracy could feel Mackenzie walking up behind her, and she knew exactly what he was going to say. She spun around and started arguing with him before he even said a word. "I know what you are thinking, and I absolutely have the authority to pull that woman off active duty in regards to ROC Three."

Mackenzie shrugged. "That's true. It's also true that I have the ability and responsibility to go over your head and have her reinstated. Just so that we understand each other, I'll go directly to the President if I have to."

Tracy took a step forward so that she and Mackenzie were almost nose to nose. "That woman feels that she is more ROC than human right now. ROC Three is not a plane or a jet. It's a living, breathing monster with thoughts and desires of its own. Right now Green's brainwaves are in complete sync with the brainwaves of that monster! Did you hear her screech when she was connected to ROC Three? She is currently lost both psychologically and emotionally. There is a very real possibility that she will give in to the ROC's whims, its natural instincts. If Green pilots ROC Three again prior to clearing a psychological evaluation, ROC Three may end up turning on us. It may attack a city or even innocent civilians. The innocent civilians that we are supposed to protect. Did you ever think about them?"

Mackenzie spoke in a slow measured tone, "Those civilians are exactly the people that I am thinking of right now. They are under a threat from creatures that they cannot possibly understand, and they are frightened of them. Amongst other countries, ROC Three is responsible for Russia, Pakistan, China, and India. There are two major factors to consider with those four countries. First, none of them are on the best terms with the U.S. If they are attacked, and we tell them that ROC Three is unavailable, they might very well cave to Rol-Hama's demands and start attacking other countries who have not given into his demands. Countries like the U.S. who has said that they had a ROC to protect them except for when our pilot is stressed out. Second, those four countries all have nuclear capabilities. What to do you think that they will do after conventional weapons fail and a giant monster is still rampaging through their cities? How many civilians do you think would die if the Chinese nuked Hong Kong? Then, of course, they could decide instead of nuking their own country, maybe they figure that Rol-Hama will call off the monster if they give into his demands and attack a country that is holding out. How big of statement would China make to Rol-Hama by firing a nuke at the U.S.?"

Tracy flopped down into her chair. "You have a lot of *ifs* in that scenario. Let me ask you, what do you think that China will do if

ROC Three attacks them because Green has given into the ROC's instinct?"

Mackenzie leaned in toward Tracy. 'Captain Green is a trained United States Navy pilot with an impeccable record. She has passed several psychological tests throughout her career. She just needs some rest, and she will be fine."

Tracy sighed. "She is a woman who is nearly crippled, and we gave the ability to feel that she is flying. She is not mentally stable for another mission, and I will not clear her for one."

Mackenzie shrugged. "Okay, then put one of the other pilots into ROC Three if the need arises."

Tracy shook her head. "It doesn't work like that. It takes months of neuro-link probes between pilot and ROC. ROC Three would not respond to another pilot, and moreover, if another pilot tried to neuro-link with ROC Three, it may disrupt the link that pilot has with his or her ROC. I can't in good conscious put ROC Three back into action until Captain Green is mentally stable enough to engage in neuro-link with her again."

Mackenzie turned and walked away. "Captain Green and ROC Three will both be activated the next time that a kaiju attacks an area under their protection. Don't worry, your conscience can be clear of this decision, because I am taking it out of your hands. Expect a direct order from the President shortly confirming everything that I just said."

Tracy began to tear up, and she put her hands in her face so that no one would see her crying. She heard a door open behind her, and she knew that it would be Crow coming back into the room to report on Green's status.

Crow could see that Tracy was upset by the events that had just occurred. Aside from the responsibility that she felt for Green and all of the pilots, Crow had also heard at least part of her argument with Mackenzie. Crow approached, Tracy sat at her computer with her hands in her face. In addition to being upset, Tracy was obviously tired and frustrated by the situation as well. Crow sat down next to her.

She turned toward him. "I get one pilot who gets too deep into the ROC's mind and one who can't connect with his ROC's instincts at all."

Crow knew that Tracy was looking for comfort but that was just not part of his makeup. He told people what they needed to hear, not what they wanted to hear. He leaned forward. "You saw what happened to Green. That's why I don't let ROC One into my mind. That's why I call the shots, and the bird follows my lead."

Tracy threw her arms out in frustration. "Bixby and Munroe get it! They sync with their ROC'S and still managed to maintain a semblance of self. Their links could be stronger with their ROCs, but why are they able to understand how to maintain that balance and you two struggle with it?"

Crow looked into Tracy's eyes. "They hump like disturbed rabbits, maybe that's the key."

A quick look of surprise at the way Crow was staring at her flashed across Tracy's face, but it was quickly replaced with a look of intrigue. "You know, Captain Crow, you just might be onto something."

The ever stoic face of Crow now had a slight look of surprise on it. He took a deep breath, and then he looked into her eyes. "Look, I think that I may need to talk to you about something of a personal nature if you have the time."

Tracy shook her head *yes* with an intense look on her face.

Crow took a deep breath, and then the alarm went off.

They looked to the monitor to see the Jersey Devil attacking Philadelphia. The demonic horror had landed in the center of the city, and it was tearing Philadelphia apart. They saw a news feed of the kaiju slashing it claws into the Comcast building.

When Crow saw the outline of bodies falling out of the side of building, he didn't wait for his name to be called. He looked Tracy directly in the eyes. "I need to talk to you about something important when I get back." Crow then ran over to his recliner and put his neuro-link helmet on. Five seconds later, ROC 1 was in the air and heading to the City of Brotherly Love to confront a demon from the darkest depths of Hell. Several seconds later, the information on the creature was fed into Crow's Neuro-Link:

Jersey Devil– a winged creature who lives in the Pine Barrens forest of New Jersey.

Descriptions – The beast is said to be a kangaroo-like creature with clawed hands, cloven hooves, the wings of a bat, and a forked tail. While reports of the creature date back to Pre-Columbian times, the most famous series of reports took place in 1909. The creature was reported to have attacked people all over the South Jersey area. It is reported to have turned over a cable car and to have attacked a social club where gunfire was unable to harm it. It slew several members of the club.

Current data from attack – The creature appears to be the same kaiju that attacked Atlantic City several days ago. It has claws, large leathery wings, cloven hooves, and a long mouth of serrated teeth. The creature is bipedal and stands 285 feet tall, and it weighs in excess of 5,000 tons. NOTE: This creature has the ability to fly. Thus far the creature has not been reported to fly at supersonic speed.

CHAPTER 11

Officer Jack Williams was doing his best to look brave as he tried to direct people into a subway entrance as a massive winged demon tore apart the statue of William Penn that stood atop of city hall. The citizens of his city were scared, and he was doing his best to be brave for them. In times of crisis, people looked to police officers to be strong, and he was not going to let them down.

Jack was staring at the monster as he continued to wave people into what he hoped was the protection of the underground subway platform. The monster had a long horse-like face that was filled with jagged teeth and long curved horns sprouting out of the back of its head. It legs looked like the twisted legs of a goat, while it had the powerful torso of a body builder. The monster had long claws for hands and ominous bat-like wings sprouting out of its back.

Every summer Jack's father would drive Jack, his sister, and their mother down to the Jersey Shore, and as they passed through a wooded area known as the *Pine Barrens*, Jack's father would tell them the story about Mrs. Leeds' thirteenth child. Jack couldn't remember all of the details—something along the lines that Mrs. Leeds was a witch who promised her thirteenth child to Satan. When the baby was born, it came out as a demon who flew up the chimney and out into the woods. Jack never believed the story, and even when the monster had attacked Atlantic City, he still thought that the creature was some kind of mutation made up by the terrorists. Now that Jack saw the monster standing before him, he was beginning to change his mind. As the monster stomped City Hall into rubble, Jack looked at the morbid creature he could actually believe was the spawn of Satan.

Jack shifted his gaze to see an elderly couple trying their best to run to the shelter of the subway station. They were moving as fast as they could, but Jack could tell that they were not going to make it. City Hall was in ruins, so the kaiju turned its attention to the hotel next to it. The hotel was starting to shake from the pounding that it was taking. Jack could see that a large chunk of concrete was about to fall on the elderly couple. Jack ran toward them and he scooped them both up. He held the man in his left arm and the woman in his right. He was squeezing them tightly, and while he was worried that he might have broken a rib or two, he figured that it was better for the elderly couple than it would have been if they were crushed to death by the crumbling building.

As Jack was trying to run he heard the Devil snarling and tearing the city asunder. Jack was trying to block out the horrible sound in his mind. He tried to focus on the sound of a whistle in his head as white noise to block out the horror that was occurring behind him. The elderly couple were thrashing in pain and fear as Jack strained to hold onto them and carry them to safety. Jack could feel his arms tiring, and he continued to focus on the whistling sound to help him make it to the subway tunnel entrance that was still over one hundred feet away from him. In Jack's head, he could hear the whistling sound growing louder and louder. He figured that he was doing a good job of focusing his mind on the sound until the old man shouted about the whistling getting louder too. It was then that Jack realized that the sound was not in his head but coming from the sky. He ran the last fifty feet to the subway tunnel and handed the banged up elderly couple to one of his fellow officers, who helped them into the subway tunnel.

He turned to see the remains of the building that the elderly couple been under crumble down onto the street. Jack breathed a quick sigh of relief knowing that he had saved their lives even if only for the moment. Jack looked up at the demonic figure of the Devil as it turned to the subway entrance, and he instantly knew that by running out to save the elderly couple that he had drawn the monster's attention. He cursed, thinking that by trying to save two people he may have just doomed hundreds to certain death.

The Devil took a step toward the subway entrance as the high pitched whistling sound continued to build. Jack looked at the Devil, and behind the kaiju, he saw a second set of wings appear. The whistling sound reached near deafening proportions as ROC 1 swooped out of the air and used its talons to rake the Devil across the face. The Devil looked up and roared at ROC 1. All of his life Jack and been a devout Catholic, and since the time he was a child, he had heard stories about how Michael the Arch Angel had thrown Satan out of Heaven and cast him into Hell.

As ROC 1 spread its feathered wings and fluttered above the Devil, and the Devil lashed at the giant bird, to Jack it felt as though the battle for Heaven between angles and demons was being replayed before him on the streets of Philadelphia. The fluttering of ROC 1's wings was causing a wind shear of near hurricane proportions. The wind blast caught the Devil's wings and sent him skidding into a building that he crashed into, which then quickly collapsed on top of him.

The force of the wind also sent Jack tumbling down the stairs to the subway entrance. When he hit the bottom of the stairs he looked back up to see ROC 1 takeoff faster than any jet he had ever seen as it streaked away from the city. Several seconds later, Jack saw the Devil take to the sky as dust and debris poured off of its body. The Jersey Devil roared in anger, and then it took off in pursuit of ROC 1.

Back in the Nest, Crow was giving updates to Mackenzie, Tracy, and Dr. Crean. "The kaiju is now in pursuit. I am still not at top speed, and the monster does not appear to be gaining. I should be able to have it follow me until we are away from a populated area."

Mackenzie shouted to Crow, "Where are you planning to engage the beast?"

"I am taking him back home to the Pine Barrens forest. The population there is extremely sparse, and I should be able to engage the target with minimal casualties and collateral damage."

Mackenzie nodded. "Good thinking, Captain. Now take that ugly bastard down."

Crow didn't respond. He knew that ROC 1 had made it over the dense forest of the Pine Barrens, and he was prepared to engage the monster. He slowed ROC 1, and then dipped to an altitude of roughly one thousand feet above the tree tops of the forest.

The Devil saw that ROC 1 had decreased in altitude and it did as well. The monster flew at ROC 1, with its mouth wide open and dripping with drool.

ROC 1 aimed itself directly at the monster, and then with a few flaps of its mighty wings, it closed the distance between the monster and itself. Crow could sense that ROC 1 wanted to meet the Devil head-on in a flash of claws and talons, but as usual, Crow blocked out any thoughts from ROC 1 as he imposed his will on the creature.

Crow had ROC 1 continue to increase its speed as the two monsters raced toward each other. While Crow did not let ROC 1's thoughts influence his own, he was well aware of the creature's capabilities and strengths. Just as the two monsters were about to collide Crow had ROC 1 pull up. Crow had timed ROC 1's increase in speed so that it was at the precise moment that ROC 1 broke the sound barrier that he passed over the kaiju.

A sonic boom exploded over the Devil. The force of the blast hammered the beast into the forest below. Hundreds of trees were crushed or thrown into the air as the Devil created a gigantic crater in the middle of the forest.

As the Devil lay stunned below it, ROC 1 felt the urge to land on top of the creature and tear it to shreds, but Crow had a different attack plan. He had ROC 1 hover several hundred feet over the creature where it dropped its diamond coated bladed feathers into the back of the monster, while at the same time covering the beast in a cloud of liquid nitrogen. The Devil writhed in pain as its body was simultaneously being cut to ribbons and frozen solid.

Much quicker than Crow would have thought possible, the Devil sprang into the air, spun around, and slashed at ROC 1 with its claw. Crow felt ROC 1 reflexively attempt to fly backward and away from the blow, but Crow's mind was in such control of ROC 1 that's its body did not obey the bird's reactions. The claw of the Devil caught ROC 1 in the area that its wing connected to its body. ROC 1 crashed into the thick forest, and Crow quickly found ROC 1 flat on its stomach with the son of Satan looming over it.

The Devil drove its hoof onto to ROC 1 wings, and then it used its claw to gash ROC 1 across its back. The cyborg screamed in pain as blood and feathers covered the green tree tops of the forest.

Despite the pain that ROC 1 was in, Crow maintained his impassive demeanor. He could hear Tracy yelling at him to let ROC 1's thoughts help guide him through the battle, and he could hear Dr. Crean screaming that ROC 1 was not capable of sustaining another blow like that.

Crow blocked out the screaming scientists and focused on fighting a battle. He had ROC 1 turn its head to the side, and then he sprayed more liquid nitrogen onto the foot and leg of the Devil. The demonic figure quickly took to the sky to avoid having its leg frozen solid. Crow forced ROC 1 to lifts its body off of the ground and take to the sky as well. Crow was well aware that in the air ROC 1 had a distinct speed and maneuverability advantage over the less aerodynamically designed Devil. Crow had ROC 1 fly a large circle to put some distance between itself and the Devil. Crow knew that a little distance would be all that he needed to slay this beast.

The animalistic Devil flew directly at ROC 1, and while ROC 1 wanted to charge again, Crow had the bird fly above the Devil and drop several more of its bladed feathers onto the monster. The Devil roared in anger, and then continued to pursue ROC 1. Crow had ROC 1 fly at a speed that kept it several hundred yards out of the Devil's reach. Crow would count in his head as they were flying, and every 90 seconds, he would have ROC 1 turn around, fly over the Devil, and then drop another barrage of bladed feathers onto the demon. Crow was aware that the feathers were not causing much damage to the Devil, but the attacks were angering the creature and encouraging him to continue his pursuit of ROC 1. Within five minutes of taking to the air, ROC 1 soared over the remains of Atlantic City, and headed out over the Atlantic Ocean, with the enraged Devil still pursuing him.

Once they were over the water, Crow kept careful track of how far out over the ocean that they had flown. Once they had cleared ten miles Crow had ROC 1 make its move. Crow had realized that ROC 1 had the advantage in speed and agility in the air, but that the Devil was far more powerful and adept on the ground than ROC 1. If he had continued to fight the Devil over land the battle would have been a long, drawn out war of attrition, with the two monsters constantly shifting as to who had the upper hand. Over the ocean, though, Crow had taken the Devil's superior size and weight and turned them into a distinct disadvantage. He directed ROC 1 to fly high over the Devil, and then as the Devil tried to pursue his nemesis, Crow had ROC 1 streak down at the monster, with its claws extended. Having learned from their exchange back in the city Crow knew that attacking the Devil's powerful jaws or body would be a mistake. As ROC 1 closed in on its prey, Crow had the bird shift slightly so that ROC 1's talons tore into the leathery flesh of the Jersey Devil's wings. ROC 1's talons hooked into the Devil's wings, and then ROC 1 began to use his beak to further rip apart the Devil's bat-like wings. The entire attack took less than five seconds, but at the end of it, the Devil was plummeting helplessly into the Atlantic Ocean. The Jersey Devil hit the ocean and roared as its body bobbed up and down on the water.

ROC 1 flew low over the Devil, where Crow then had it empty the remains of its liquid nitrogen reserves onto the beast and the water around it. The Devil howled in fear as its body began to be incased in ice. Within seconds, the Devil's massive head and one of its arms were trapped in a huge iceberg as its legs and tail thrashed in vain in the water beneath it. Crow had ROC 1 circle the frozen monster, and he watched through the bird's enhanced eyes as the Devil slowly suffocated. Once the Devil had ceased its thrashing Crow directed ROC 1 to fly back to shore. As ROC 1 was flying, its keen eyes caught the site of a massive Great White Shark below it. Crow could tell that the beast was hungry, and for the briefest moment, he let ROC 1 be in control of its body. ROC 1 scooped the twenty five foot shark out of the ocean as easily as an eagle would a trout from a stream. ROC 1 dropped the large predator onto the beach of Atlantic City where Crow let it devour the fish before flying back to Texas.

CHAPTER 12

The Nest

Bixby ordered another beer as he and Munroe sat at the pilots' bar and watched the feed from Crow's neuro-link as it played across the screens throughout the Nest. Normally, they would have been at the neuro-link station, but after what had happened to Green, they each silently felt the need to get away from situation for a little bit. They both cheered when they saw that Crow and ROC 1 had defeated the Jersey Devil. Bixby smiled a little while in his head, he could hear Crow chiding them for cheering because he had just done his job and that there was still a war to be fought.

He looked over at Munroe, who was still watching the feed of the battle on the screen as it started to replay itself. He and Munroe often sat together when they had a drink or grabbed a bite to eat. They even talked to each other about what they had recently done on their last flight or they simply joked around or flirted with each other, but they never really talked about anything of any substance. Bixby knew that this was a conscious choice on both of their parts. They were both career military people. The only true love that each of them had ever had was with flying and the sky. Bixby also knew how different that they were from other people that they typically interacted with. Each of them was far superior to almost any other pilot on the planet. Comparing them to ace fighter pilots was like comparing an all-star basketball player to Michael Jordan or LeBron James. Other pilots were good but they were simply not in the same class as he and Munroe. Top notch pilots had the ability to think their way through a battle or dire situation, but he and Munroe were able to simply react to a situation and overcome it. That's what made them so much better than everyone else.

At the same time, it was these very attributes that kept them distant from everyone else. Bixby had only a small handful of friends in high school from his baseball team, and then really no friends when he joined the academy or when he became an active pilot. Sure, people talked to him and admired him, but none of them saw the world as he did, or flew as well as he did either. They simply did not have the ability to do so. He and Munroe had never spoken about it, but he suspected that her experiences were similar to his own. That because her talent was so far beyond everyone around her that she too was an outsider.

That feeling of being disconnected and superior to the majority of his peers was something that Bixby had learned to live with, and in many ways, he looked at it with a sense of pride. Recently though, he was beginning to rethink his approach to dealing with other people. His reasons for doing so came directly from his neuro-link with ROC 3 and his interactions with his fellow ROC pilots, in particular, Crow and Green.

When he had first met Crow, Bixby had admired him. The man was a top notch pilot who did not take crap from anyone and who was solely focused on his mission. Bixby often thought that he would one day become what Crow was, and at first, he was thrilled by the idea but now that thought almost scared him.

Crow had no friends, no family, and no one who he could interact with—including ROC 1. They had all seen the brainwave scans from their various test flights, and it was obvious that Crow and ROC 1 were not syncing at all. Bixby himself had a decent sync with ROC 4. It was not a great sync but the neuro-link was strong, and he and ROC 4 were able to have some give-and-take from each other's skill sets.

When Bixby had first entered the program he and ROC 4 were barely syncing at all. Several weeks into the program the sync improved a good deal. Dr. Curry thought that the improved sync was due to the hours of time that he and ROC 4 had logged together, but Bixby knew that there was as another explanation. His sync had improved when he and Munroe had started having sex. It was just sex, and at first, Bixby only looked at Munroe as a hot piece of ass that he could have a mutually beneficial arrangement with. When he started to sync better with ROC 4, the thought began to creep into his mind that maybe there was more to it. Even though his interactions with Munroe were purely physical, it was a connection to another human, and that connection helped him sync better with ROC 4 because his thought process was slowly changing to the point where understanding and interacting with another living creature was something that he was open to. Bixby was sure that Crow had long ago passed the point where that type of connection was possible, and that was why he was totally out of sync with ROC 1. Crow was able to control ROC 1 but that was because the man was basically a Terminator. He was almost a soulless robot who was totally focused on his mission. When Bixby realized this he began to question if Crow really was the man that he wanted to become.

As Bixby's sync with ROC 4 became stronger, he began to look at the bird as more than just a weapon or a monster. He actually began to look at ROC 4 as a friend, and he realized that through the neuro-link that ROC 4 actually knew him better than any human on the planet. Bixby was good with that, though. He looked at ROC 4 as he would a co-pilot during war time. ROC 4 should know him better than anyone else because their connection could kill monsters, stop terrorist, and most importantly, save lives.

He had looked to Sheena Green to see this belief reaffirmed. Green was another person who had no friends or family, but unlike Crow, she seemed to enjoy her life here at the Nest. Green was almost in total sync with ROC 3, and Bixby had thought that her ability to sync with ROC 3 meant that she was capable of forming and maintaining healthy relationships with people. Today's events had shattered Bixby's conceptions about Green. He thought that it was Green's ability to form relationships that helped her sync with ROC 3, but the opposite was true. Green had almost totally withdrawn into her own mind and self-pity. To Green, her neuro-link with ROC 3 was like a drug that helped her to escape reality. The strength of her neuro-link with ROC 3 was not the type of relationship that someone drew strength and grew from. It was not the type of emotional and psychological understanding shared between a pilot and co-pilot, or best friends, or a husband and wife. Green's relationship with ROC 3 was the type of relationship that a junkie had with heroin. They looked to be in sync with each other but what Green was really doing was escaping into ROC 3. She was not fostering a partnership.

Bixby did not want to become Green either. He wanted to have a sync with ROC 4 that made him as efficient at his job as possible, but he did not want ROC 4 to be his only connection to another living being. He did not want to live for ROC 4, he wanted to live for and with other people who in turn wanted to live for and with him.

As all of these thoughts weighed down on Bixby's mind, as he continued to stare at Munroe, and for the first time he wondered if he could share these thoughts with her. He wondered if she shared these thoughts or if she would totally reject them. He knew that at first he saw Munroe as strictly a sex buddy, and he feared that maybe she only saw him as that as well.

Munroe turned toward him and found him staring at her. She smiled. "I know by the way you are looking at me exactly what you are thinking."

Bixby's face lit up. "Really?"

Munroe put her hand between his legs. "Yes, finish your beer and meet me in my room, and then we can make those thoughts a reality." She licked her lips and walked away from the bar.

For the first time in his life, Bixby was actually disappointed at being offered sex with a smoking hot woman.

Tracy Curry hung up the phone and cursed in frustration. Mackenzie had held true to his word. He had contacted the President, who had just called Tracy and ordered her to put Sheena Green back on active duty. She was cleared to counsel Green as much as she felt was needed in between missions, but Green was to be neuro-linked to ROC 3 and in the air the next time that a cryptid attacked Russia or Asia. Tracy looked at her watch. She had less than twenty hours until the next wave of kaiju-sized cryptids started attacking major cities, and that time frame was based on a terrorist being true to his word. She took a deep breath and headed for Green's quarters.

When Tracy made her way to Green's room, she knocked, but there was no answer. After knocking twice more, she used her administrative access to open the door to Green's quarters. Tracy's heart sunk when she saw Green limping around the room in a circle and crying with her arms straight out by her sides. She looked like a kid who was pretending to fly, but Tracy knew that in her mind Green was not pretending. She was still experiencing what it was like to be linked with ROC 3.

Tracy tried to get her attention. "Captain Green." Green continued to fly around the room, and Tracy tried once more to get her attention. "Captain Green, it's Dr. Curry. Please let me know if you can hear me."

Green flew one more time around the room and let out another ear piercing screech. Tracy jumped in front of Green and stopped her dead in her tracks.

"Sheena, it's me, Tracy. Please try to focus on my voice!"

Green stopped and looked at Tracy as tears continued to pour from her eyes. "Tracy, I was back in the sky! I was flying again. I was going over Moscow, the city was beautiful from above—"

"Sheena, you didn't fly over Moscow. ROC Three flew over there several days ago. You were just remembering what you saw through your neuro-link."

Green shook her head. "No, it was me. *I* was flying over Moscow! I am ROC Three. I am the ruler of the skies."

Tracy forced her to sit down. "You are Sheena Green. You are a pilot who through a neuro-link helps to guide ROC Three."

Green screeched again, and then started shouting at Tracy. "No, Sheena Green was a pathetic cripple with nothing to live for. She has no friends, no husband, no children, no one to remember her. I am ROC Three. I have the entire sky. I soar through the air and protect the world from monsters and madmen. I am a hunter who provides for my fellow birds of prey. The world needs me."

Tracy shook her head in disappointment. She wasn't disappointed in Green so much as she was disappointed in herself. Tracy leaned over and looked into Green's eyes. "Sheena, this is my fault. I should have realized what exposing someone with your history to a neuro-link with a ROC could do to your psyche." She hugged Green. "Listen to me, you are *not* ROC Three, you are Sheena Green, and you have a lot to live for. You have friends. I am your friend. I will be here whenever you need me. Sheena, you are one of the people who protects the world and saves lives. Without you, ROC Three would just be a monster. It's you, Sheena Green, who influences ROC Three to use its amazing abilities to fight monsters. It's you, Sheena Green, who use ROC Three to save lives. It's you, Sheena Green, who influences ROC Three to save the world."

Green finally put her arms around Tracy and hugged her back. "But it's ROC Three that allows a woman with a lame leg to fly and that's all that I have."

The two women sat in silence as they continued to hug each other. Tracy was at least happy that she had gotten Green to refer to herself as a separate entity from ROC 3. Tracy kept whispering into Green's ear, "You are Sheena Green. You are my friend, and I love you." She hoped that by continually saying Green's name that it would help her maintain her sense of identity.

Crow was again working out in his room. He continued to scan the internet for any information that he could find on cryptids located in North and South America. He read descriptions of a Mothman, a Goatman, Phantom Panthers, and the Chupacabra. His main focus though was on the giant Bigfoot or Sasquatch that had attacked San Jose. Crow had evidence that the creature was real and under the control of Rol-Hama. He did not doubt that down the line he would be leading ROC 1 into a confrontation with the powerful kaiju.

He was also watching all of Rol-Hama's latest video in a loop. He could tell that the man was a fanatic, not only in regards to the Thuggee, but in every aspect of his life. His physical appearance told Crow that he took a good deal of time to exercise. The man was jacked, but Crow could tell that it was a natural build. Rol-Hama was well muscled but it was proportionate to his frame. The man was not using steroids or other enhancements. The videos were all shot in a dark room with no windows to give an idea where the Thuggee cult might be hiding. Crow knew that Mackenzie had a team of people in the CIA and NSA working on finding Rol-Hama and combing these videos, but Crow didn't trust anyone but himself. He needed to scan the videos in case those computer nerds at the NSA missed something that a man who had been in the field may pick up on.

From the one video that showed Rol-Hama's skin, Crow had guessed that he was probably somewhere in the Middle East. This was safe bet since it was an easy area for terrorists to hide in but it really didn't help narrow anything down. Crow continued to study the videos trying to see if Rol-Hama had used a particular phrase or terminology that would clue Crow into where the terrorist was, but Rol-Hama was smart. He didn't let anything slip that would give away his location. After scanning the videos for a clue from Rol-Hama, he began to look at the room itself. There were things that even the most careful of planners could not account for, and

Crow was determined to find the small thing that Rol-Hama had missed in his video that would give him away. Crow scanned the walls to see exactly what type of material that they were constructed with. He scanned to the floor to see if there was any of the terrain from the area tracked into the room where the video was made, but he could see that Rol-Hama had the room carefully cleaned to account for this.

There was not much else that Rol-Hama had left Crow or anyone else to work with. Rol-Hama had made sure that the image on the video was mainly filled up by his head and torso, with only the smallest bit of the room anywhere in view. Crow shifted his eyes to the ceiling of the video. He was watching it carefully when he saw a small black dot move a fraction of an inch on the ceiling. Crow rewound the video and played it again, and once more, he saw the black dot move a fraction of an inch. He used his tablet to focus on the spot. Then, he enlarged the area and played the few seconds of video again. This time when Crow was watching the video he smiled, and said, "Hello there, Maprissa Muscoa, you jumpy little bastard." Crow saved the image and gathered the information he had also amassed on two separate fatal car accidents. With all of the data that he had gathered finally coming together, Crow went in search of Mackenzie.

CHAPTER 13

Rol-Hama stood in front of his followers again, with the statue of Kali standing behind him. He had just slain the two men who were responsible for unleashing the Monkey Man and the Jersey Devil. Since the creatures died, the men who were responsible for them had died as well. Rol –Hama held the sword that he had used to gut the men in front of his gathered followers, and then he licked the blood off of the sword. He turned to his followers with an enraged look on his face. "The people of the world have not responded to our demands. They continue to use the Garudas to fight off our monsters. They feel that these birds of Vishnu can protect them, but we will show them that they are wrong! We have tried to give the people of the world the chance to acknowledge Kali as the one true god by only having two of our creatures attack at a given time. At the conclusion of the next time period, we shall unleash all of the creatures that we have captured and enlarged. We shall see how numerous the Garudas of Vishnu are. I doubt that they will be able to answer all of our challenges. Six hours from now millions will die. Six hours from now several cities shall be reduced to rubble." Rol-Hama took a deep breath and let silence hang over the room for several seconds before he screamed out the final part of his proclamation, "Seven hours from now the leaders of the world will realize that they have no choice but to accept Kali as the one true god. Seven hours from now I will be Kali's representative on Earth and ruler of the world. You men shall also know power as you help me to carry Kali's commands across the planet."

The gathered Thuggee first began to chant the name of *Kali*, but the chant quickly changed to *Rol-Hama*. The charismatic and fearsome leader dismissed his followers, and then he once more entered the hidden cell behind the statue of Kali. He still held the bloody sword in his hand when he saw Dr. Branson and Dr. Teig sitting sullenly in their cells. They were both staring at the video feed of their respective families.

Rol-Hama walked to a seat in between their two cells and turned off the feed to their families. He smiled at the scientists. "Gentlemen, the lists that you have provided me with were extremely helpful in determining not only who has created the massive birds which have fought against my kaiju, but it has even helped me to narrow down where they are located." The cult leader brought up the lists of names of former students that the two scientists had given to him. He brought three names from Teig's list and two from Branson's list onto the screen. "From the names that you provided of students who could have accomplished these tasks, only these five individuals went to work for the military."

Rol-Hama then brought the names of Tracy Curry and Jillian Crean to the forefront of the screen. "The other individuals are working on various projects for the military in different parts of the world but nothing that would indicate that they were creating giant monsters or the technology to control them. These two, however, Dr. Curry and Dr. Crean, there is no information on them other than the fact that they joined military research and defense, and then they seem to have disappeared." Rol-Hama laughed. "The American military think that they do such a fine job of hiding their top scientists, but did you know that last year the parents of both Dr. Curry and Dr. Crean were flown into separate cities in the American Mid-West at Christmas time? Dr. Curry's family was flown into Missouri, and Dr. Crean's family was flown into Colorado." Rol-Hama brought a map of the United States up onto the screen. "It is noteworthy that the great state of Kansas is located between these two states."

Rol-Hama hit another key on his computer and dozens of red dots appeared on the screen. "As you know, my followers and I have spent the better part of two decades hunting down various cryptids, that with your help, we now have enlarged, enhanced, and control. We were able to find many of the cryptids, but one that constantly eluded us, was the legendary Thunderbird. The massive winged creatures have been spotted all over the country, but you will see a small cluster in the American Mid-West. When we were searching for these creatures we surmised that these large birds must be nesting at the tops of mountains that were nearly inaccessible to humans. Sadly, we were never able to find the Thunderbirds."

Rol-Hama laughed. "The thought had never occurred to me that perhaps we were not the only ones creating giant monsters. All of that time looking for a massive bird nest when what I should have been looking for was a large series of buildings or hangars in the Mid-West that could hold government created Garudas."

His visage quickly changed from a jovial appearance to one of deadly anger. "How long do you think that my Mothman will have to fly over Kansas before he is able to locate a massive base, and then attack it? Do not think that your pupils' Garudas will be able to protect them either. Tomorrow we launch an all-out assault on the people of Earth. Those massive birds will be engaged with numerous threats."

The scientists were silent as they both feared for the lives of their students.

Rol-Hama could see the fear in their eyes. He smiled at them. "Do not fear, gentlemen. Your students will not be slain. They possess skills far greater than your own, and they can be of use to me. The Mothman shall locate the base and attack it. While he has the defenses of the base engaged with him, my followers shall enter the building and abduct these women." Rol-Hama stood. "You gentlemen should be proud. There is no greater honor that a teacher can receive than to be surpassed by his student." He turned the video screen back to the families of the two doctors. "No, gentlemen, do not fear for your students, rather fear for yourselves and your families."

Dr. Teig shouted, "Wait, what are you talking about? You said that if we gave you the names of our students that you would spare our families."

Rol-Hama screamed, "You have failed both me and Kali! The kaiju that you have created for me are inferior to the beasts created and controlled by your students. The punishment for failing is death, but you men are also responsible for training those who would create the beasts which would challenge Kali! Death will come to you, but it will not be until after you have suffered by watching your wives become my concubines and your children become my followers."

Branson yelled, "Your reasoning is insane! How could we possibly have known that our students would use their skills to create monsters for a war that we could never have anticipated?"

Rol-Hama screamed, "It is not my reasoning! It is the will of Kali! In the mass confusion of the coming attacks, your families shall be taken from their homes and brought here. Take a good look at them now, for you shall not see them again until their wills have been broken and they are completely subservient to me. Once you see that I have broken them, then you will die!"

CHAPTER 14

Glasgow, Scotland

A long black serpentine body with two relatively small sets of legs undulated through the water off the coast of Glasgow. The creature had been in a holding pattern in the waters of the Atlantic for several days ever since it had used the underground tunnels from the loch to access the open ocean. The serpent had fed on several species of whale as it swam up and down the coast awaiting its next command. The creature was starting to become hungry again, and when it sensed a pod of Humpback whales nearby, it began to swim after them until it received a command in its mind to turn and head to land. The long, thick body of the creature swam to the surface of the ocean. When its eyes pierced the surface it looked at the city of Glasgow. It was the middle of the night and normally the bright lights of the city would have caused the timid creature to shy away from the metropolis and its inhabitants, but the chip that had been implanted into the creature's brain urged it to attack the city.

Nessie had always been a peaceful creature that swam back and forth from the ocean to Loch Ness on a regular basis. The monster had always been careful to avoid humans at any cost, but that was prior to the Thuggee capturing the creature and altering it through surgery and genetic manipulation. The once peaceful Nessie now had a length of over four hundred feet. Now the creature was spurred on by the rage that the Thuggee had planted inside of it. The beast roared as it swam toward Glasgow harbor.

Several fishing ships were the first to see the large swell of water heading toward land, proclaiming the approach of another monster. As the beast entered the harbor the fishing ships were tossed around in the wake of the massive kaiju. At this point, the entire world knew that the Thuggee were using monsters to attack cities around the world. Several of the ships radioed into shore about the quickly approaching kaiju, but their warnings were in vain.

Nessie slithered ashore crushing most of the docks on the harbor as she crawled onto land. The beast hissed and destroyed several warehouses as she made her way deeper into the city. Nessie entered the heart of the city where she wrapped her long body around a tall building. When her body had made its way to the top of the structure, she constricted her muscles like a giant python, and tons of steel and concrete gave way under her incredible power. The monster fell back into the streets amongst the rubble and dust that she had created.

Dozens of police cars had quickly arrived to try and contain the monster until the military could arrive and battle the creature. Captain MacDougal was in charge of the police response to the crisis. As MacDougal jumped out of his car, the brave men and woman of the Glasgow police department followed his lead with little more than shotguns to battle a creature larger than a blue whale, and nearly impervious to modern weapons. MacDougal knew that his officers could not possibly stop the monster. He only hoped that they could occupy it long enough so that as many people as possible could be evacuated from the immediate area. Captain MacDougal grabbed a megaphone and pointed at the towering monster as he addressed his officers, "All right, officers. We are the only thing standing between that monster and the people of Glasgow. I won't lie to you, we won't be able to stop it. All that we can hope to do is delay it long enough to let the evacuation vehicles move people away from that thing as quickly as possible." He took a deep breath. "I know that many of you have families at home, if anyone of you wishes to leave to be with them, you will not face any consequences either professionally or personally." He waited for a moment, and he was filled with pride as each of his officers stood his or her ground. MacDougal shouted, "All right, officers. Let's save some lives!" The streets of Glasgow were lit up in orange flames as the gathered officers fired in unison at the beast that until today most of Scotland had seen as a loveable folktale.

The officer's bullets bounce off the thick hide of Nessie. The shotguns had done little more to the monster than gain her attention. Nessie hissed at the swirling lights of the police cars showering them in a mix of salvia and rotting fish remains. After she had spat her challenge at her attackers, her body moved like lightning as she slithered through the cars and the officers standing beside them. She crushed everything in her path as if it were made of cardboard. After the snake-like monster had plowed through the police force, she began to wrap her long body around a second building. Moments later, she constricted her body once more turning another building into dust. The monster plowed straight through the base of another building as she continued to spread her reign of destruction across the city.

London, England

No one was really sure how the attacked commenced. Some people say that the creature came falling out of the sky as if he had leaped a great distance like The Incredible Hulk in the movies. Still other people say that it started in the subway as a figure in a long black cloak threw his cape to the ground, grew to an enormous height, and tore through the street itself. It then climbed out of the crater and began burning the city to ashes.

Paul Richards didn't know how the attack had started. All that he cared about right this second was that he had a bus full of kids that were his responsibility. This responsibility weighed heavy on him as he was looking through his windshield at a giant with a demonic face, steel clawed hands, tattered black clothes, and some kind of metal helmet on top of its head. The creature slashed his claw into a nearby billboard, and his steel clawed hand cut the large advertisement into five separate pieces. The demonic figure turned to look at Paul's bus, and the second that Paul saw the beast's fearsome glowing eyes, he threw the bus into reverse. He plowed through several cars that were behind him causing a massive pile up of vehicles.

Paul had no sooner hit the first car that was behind his bus and pushed it back onto the curb than the spot where his bus was a moment ago exploded in blue flames. Paul first looked back to see if all the children on his bus were safe and he was glad to see that they were. He then looked back through his windshield to see the gigantic figure bend his knees, and then leap high into the air easily clearing the London skyline with room to spare. The horrifying creature landed several blocks over where it once more began to spit fire onto the buildings of London. Paul ushered the students out of the back of the bus and away from the flames in front of him. He was relieved to see that the driver of the car that he had slammed into and pushed out of the way crawling out from behind an air bag.

Most of the kids were crying and looking to him for guidance. There was a young boy standing next to him, who asked, "Mr. Richards, what was that thing?"

Paul looked at the young boy. "When I was a kid my dad told me the legend of a mysterious figure known as *Spring-Heeled Jack*. I am pretty sure that was him." Paul then rushed the kids to under the awning of the nearest building and out of the panicked streets.

St. Petersburg, Russia

A blizzard pounded the city of St. Petersburg. Roughly a foot of snow had already covered the city and more than another foot was expected to fall in the next hour alone. Oleg Zaroff was carefully steering his plow truck through the streets of St. Petersburg. He knew full well that he would have to make another pass over this area by the time that he had finished his section of the city, but that was fine with him. Oleg was paid by the hour and the cold didn't bother him. So, a second sweep meant more money for him. He was also pleased that he worked the northern most outskirts of the city. In this section of the city, the population was sparse, and the streets were wide so that even with a near blinding snow hitting his windshield he could drive slow enough to clear the streets and not really have to worry about hitting anything.

He turned a corner and headed for one of the most remote streets of the edge of the city. Without many buildings in the area, Oleg could only see a few meters in front of his truck. He was cruising along at a slow speed when he crashed into something that brought his truck to a complete stop. The backend of his truck lifted up into the air, and then came crashing down. Oleg was actually relieved that his truck had come to a dead stop. A complete stop meant that he had hit an object and not a person or an animal. Had he hit anything short of an escaped elephant the truck would have literally plowed right through whatever he had hit. With the blizzard, Oleg couldn't see through his windshield, so he climbed out of his truck to see what he had run over. As he got out of his truck all that he could see was a brown wall in front of him. At first, Oleg thought that he must have lost the road and hit the side of building. The snow plow driver realized how wrong his assumption was when the wall started to lift up in front of him.

Oleg looked up into the heavy snow, and as his gaze went up, he became aware that what he thought was a wall was actually a gargantuan foot. The foot lifted up into the sky, and as it did so, Oleg saw an incredibly thick leg. The leg looked almost human except that even with its huge size taken into account, the leg was far too thick for a human. As the owner of the leg stepped forward its towering body momentarily blocked the falling snow. Oleg gasped as he beheld a two hundred foot tall semi-human. The creature had broad shoulders and long powerful arms. The face looked somewhat human except for its protruding brow and flat nose. Oleg thought for a moment that the creature looked like a giant Neanderthal.

As the giant walked past him and headed for the city, Oleg remembered reports that he had heard about terrorists capturing monsters from around the world and causing them to grow to huge proportions, and then unleashing them on cities. As Olaf watched the giant heading for St. Petersburg, he whispered the word, "Almas."

Sydney

Charlie and Kristy Buonno were enjoying their vacation in Australia despite the turmoil occurring around the world. When the Bunyip had attacked Melbourne they had initially thought about returning home to Maine, but when they had heard that giant monster or *kaiju* attacks were taking place all over the world, they figured that they were as safe in Sydney as they were anywhere else. They had reasoned that they had already spent the money for their trip to the *Land Down Under* and now they were going have a good time no matter what. Besides, if the world was going to be overrun with giant cryptids, then this might be the last chance that they had to travel abroad for the rest of their lives.

The couple walked through streets, and Charlie used his new digital camera to take pictures of every landmark that they came across. They had stopped at the Darlinghurst Theater and Charlie was taking a picture of it when the building exploded in front of them. The couple ran away from the falling chunks of concrete when the building across the street also exploded. Charlie and Kristy saw, desks, cubicles, papers, and even people go flying into the air and then come crashing down into the street. The stunned couple was standing in the middle of the street with dozens of other people when another building at the end of the street exploded as well.

Charlie grabbed his wife's hand and ran into a nearby park.

Kristy yelled, "What are you doing? We need to find cover! There are buildings coming down everywhere!"

Another building exploded as Charlie said, "Yes, buildings are exploding and we don't know which building is next, so an open area is the safest place for us!" The ground shook as a building to left side of the park burst apart. Charlie turned to his wife. "There are no flames or heat, they can't be using bombs or missiles. It's almost like something is just smashing through the buildings like a giant wrecking ball.

Kristy grabbed the camera from her husband. "Charlie, take a look at the camera. You took a picture just as the theater exploded. Maybe you caught something."

Another building exploded to the right of the park as Charlie scrolled back through his pictures to see a huge red colored rod with a thin fin-like membrane wrapped around it smashing through the theater. He looked at his wife. "What in the hell is that?"

Baltimore, Maryland

Jessica Biddle took her position at the front of the boat as the last of the tourists climbed aboard for their two hour tour of the inner harbor. Jessica pulled her Ravens hat down over her head. The football game would be starting in six hours, and she figured that she could get through this tour and meet her friends for a least a couple hours of tailgating before the game started. The captain of the ship was a good looking guy who she had been flirting with back and forth throughout the summer and early fall. She decided that it was finally time to make her move. His name was Tom, and as he was revving up the boat's engine.

She leaned over and whispered to him, "If you can cut fifteen minutes off this tour I have an extra ticket to the Ravens game—if you are interested."

Tom smiled. "I can take off twenty and the hell with anyone who complains."

Jessica smiled. "Maybe the Ravens aren't the only ones who will score tonight."

Tom revved the engine hard as he smiled from ear to ear, and then pulled the boat into the harbor.

As the boat pulled away from the dock, Jessica began her speech, "Ladies and gentlemen, let me welcome you to Baltimore's world famous inner harbor. Today we will take a tour of the harbor where we will see not only the many tourist attractions around the harbor but also the wide variety of ocean life found in the bay. If you have any questions please feel free to simply raise your hand as ask. I will answer any and all questions to the best of my ability."

An elderly man in the back of the boat raised his hand.

Jessica smiled, as in her mind, she could not believe that someone had a question already. She pointed at the old man. "Yes sir, what is your question?"

The old man pointed out into the bay at several black and white shapes that slid in and out of the water. "What are those things?"

Jessica turned her gaze toward the bay, and a look of surprise came across her face. "Wow, what a treat! Those appear to be a pod of five orcas, or what are commonly known as, *killer whales*." She walked to the side of the ship that the orcas were on, and then she began informing the passengers about the animals. "The term *killer whale* is actually a misnomer, as the orcas are more closely related to porpoises than they are to whales. The orcas do occasionally enter the bay to feed, but it rarely happens. This is a real treat."

The old man raised his hand again, and Jessica sighed as she pointed to him. "Yes sir, do you have another question about the orcas?"

The old man shook his head. "No, I know what orcas are. I wanted to know what those things *behind* the orcas are."

Jessica thought the old man must be senile, but she humored him and took a second look. She dropped her microphone from her hand as she saw three rows of thick green fins sticking out of the water and following the orcas. The green fins were closing in on the orcas as the powerful animals continued to swim farther into the bay itself. A moment later, a huge swell of water began to form behind the fleeing orcas, and as the water cleared, Jessica and the passengers on the cruise ship screamed as the fins rose out of the water to reveal a gigantic saurian head.

The jaws of the awesome creature opened to show several rows of long sharp teeth. The jaws closed around two of the orcas, and it chomped the terrified animals down in two bites. The three remaining orcas swam past the tour boat as they continued to head to the shore. The saurian head rose out of the bay as the beast that it was connected to entered shallow water. As the creature rose from the bay, Jessica could finally see it clearly.

The monster's head looked reptilian, T- Rex dinosaur-like, with the long fins running across it. The shape of the body was humanoid, but it was covered in green scales. The kaiju's arms and legs both ended in menacing claws. The creature also had a long and thick tail protruding out of its back.

One of the passengers on the ship yelled out something about a Lizard Man.

Jessica didn't catch anything else that the man had said, but she could see that the monstrous lizard was on a direct collision course with the tour boat. She gripped Tom's shoulder, and screamed, "Move, Tom! Move the boat! That thing is coming right for us!"

Tom shifted the boat to full speed, and it lurched forward—throwing Jessica and anyone else who was standing, to the floor. The boat shot forward, but the Lizard Man was closing too quickly for the boat to totally clear the monster's path.

As the Lizard Man made his way past the boat, his long claw clipped the back—crushing the engine and the rear of the deck. Tom called an immediate *abandon ship*.

All the passengers were wearing lifejackets, so as they jumped into the water, they floated to the top.

Tom managed to grab Jessica in one hand and a lifejacket in the other. He jumped into the bay and held tightly onto Jessica. The two turned around to see the three remaining orcas beach themselves in the shallow water of the bay. The giant Lizard Man walked up to the squirming orcas and picked the three multi-ton beasts up with one of his claws. He lifted the squealing animals to his mouth, and then he swallowed them whole.

Jessica and Tom watched in disbelief as the Lizard Man entered the city and began attacking everything in its path. Buildings crumbled and vehicles were tossed into the air as the Lizard Man rampaged through the city. Tom looked over at Jessica. "Should I swim to shore?"

Jessica shook her head. "No, I think that we are safer in the bay. Just hold me, Tom. Hold me until this nightmare is over, and then when the monster is gone, we can make our way to what's left of the city."

San Diego Zoo

The Elephants kept running around their enclosure in a circle like they were looking for a way out. Craig Stevenson was just an undergrad interning at the zoo, but he knew odd animal behavior when he saw it. Seeing the elephants running around their pen in the same way that sheep did when a predator was nearby, definitely qualified as odd. Seeing sheep being scared was one thing, but seeing elephants scared was something else. They were elephants, after all, and there was nothing that should scare them. The pachyderms suddenly began trumpeting as they continued to circle around their pen.

Craig was about to call the zoo's vet to see if maybe he had an idea of what was wrong with them, when he suddenly heard a ruckus erupt from the rest of the animals all over the zoo. All the animals suddenly started roaring, bleating, and calling out in various sounds. It was as if all of them suddenly became scared at the same time.

Then Craig felt the ground shake underneath and it hit him: *earthquake.* He was not a native to California, and he had never experienced and earthquake before, but he knew that animals usually sensed these sorts of things before people did, and an earthquake certainly qualified as something that would scare elephants.

The shaking stopped as quickly as it started, and Craig felt a wave of relief that it was over. Then the earth shook again and a much larger wave a fear than the fear of an earthquake ran through Craig's mind. The news had said that when the giant Bigfoot had attacked San Jose that people initially thought that it was an earthquake until they realized that the shaking was really impact tremors from the giant walking.

The elephants trumpeted and began charging their gate when a horrible smell finally hit Craig's nostrils. It smelled like a garbage dump had been put behind the zoo. As the elephants broke through their pen Craig ran after them. He recalled that a horrible smell was also reported to accompany the Bigfoot in San Jose. Craig was in a full sprint when he heard a deafening roar behind him. The intern didn't turn around, he just keep running until he saw a massive fur covered leg step over him and directly into the path of the stampeding elephants. The terrified creatures continued to charge, and all five elephants rammed into the foot of the three hundred foot tall Sasquatch. The force of the elephants would have knocked a locomotive over, but the Sasquatch's foot was unmoved.

The cryptid reached down and picked up two elephants in each hand. He bit the heads off the elephants in his right hand. The blood from the animals sprayed across the primate's face and chest covering its thick fur in gore. The beasts in his left hand struggled in vain to escape the monster's powerful grip.

Craig turned around and tried to run back into the elephant's pen. He was trying to run into their indoor enclosure in hopes he could ride out the attack in there. Craig had taken three steps when he saw a huge shadow fall over him. He barely had time to scream as the largest foot in the world came crashing down on top of him.

CHAPTER 15

The Nest

Alarms blared throughout the Nest calling all of the pilots to the neuro-link station. Mackenzie, Tracy Curry, and Dr. Crean were already at their stations preparing to monitor the ROCs and the pilots as they flew into battle.

Bixby and Munroe were the first pilots to come sprinting into the neuro-links station. As the two young pilots jumped into their recliners, Mackenzie called out instructions, "All hell has broken loose. We have six kaiju attacking six different sites simultaneously!" He addressed the attacks in the United Kingdom first, "Munroe, you have two attacks occurring in your area. The first attack is taking place in London, England. The second attack is occurring in Glasgow, Scotland. Get ROC Two into the air. From its current location, it will reach London first. Information will be sent you en route to the target. After you have taken care of the target in London, we will send you instructions regarding Glasgow. The Royal Air Force will engage the target in Scotland and try to keep it from destroying the city until ROC Two can get there."

Munroe didn't respond, she just brought up her neuro-link and sent ROC 2 to London.

Bixby had ROC 4 in the air when Mackenzie called out his assignment, "Bixby, Sydney is being torn to pieces by a cryptid moving faster than the human eye can register. You are going to need to rely on ROC Four's enhanced vision to track the target. Get there ASAP! Our projections indicate that at the current rate the cryptid is destroying Sydney that there won't be anything left of it within the next hour.

Bixby yelled out, "Just send me the information on what we are dealing with. If I can't see it I am going to need to know all that I can about it."

Mackenzie nodded. "Roger that, Captain. I will send all of the information that we have on the cryptid as soon as I finish handing out assignments."

Green came limping into the neuro-link station, with a smile of utter satisfaction stretched across her face.

Tracy looked at Mackenzie, who was glaring at her and shaking his head. The scientist ignored the director's warning and ran over to Green. She put her hands on Green's shoulders and established eye contact. "Sheena, you don't have to do this. You're not ready to link with ROC Three again. It's too soon. You need to be comfortable with who you are before you open yourself up to ROC Three again."

Green just kept smiling. "It's okay. I know who I am. I know that I am needed, and I know what is expected of me." She hugged the doctor. "I'll be fine, Tracy. Thank you for all that you have done for me." Green limped past Tracy.

Tracy was unsure of what the comment about thanking her for *all that she had done for her* meant. What Tracy was sure of, was that Green's mental state was in no condition to engage in a neuro-link with ROC 3. Tracy looked to her left to see Mackenzie staring bullets at her. Tracy knew from the look on his face that she would be hearing from him and probably the President as well in regards to Green. She didn't care about either of those two consequences. She was a doctor, and Green was her under her care. She had taken an oath to always look out for the interests of her patients. Tracy told herself that the power to stop Green from neuro-linking with ROC 3 had been taken from her and that all she could do was warn Green. If Green chose to ignore those warnings, then it was the same as the smoker who was told that she had cancer and yet kept on smoking. Tracy sighed in despair as she walked back to her station.

When Green was in her recliner she pulled the neuro-link over her head. She was instantly linked with ROC 3, and once again, Green screeched as if she were a bird of prey.

Tracy stood up from her chair, but Mackenzie motioned for her to sit back down. He then called out to Green, "Moscow is under attack. They are also in the middle of a blizzard, so flying ROC Three in those conditions could be difficult. It's a dangerous mission, but we can't rule out that the Russians won't resort to nuclear weapons if we can't stop that thing, so this mission must be successful. Like the others I will send you information on the monster when you are en route. You and ROC Three can handle this, Green. Go and kick that monster's ass!"

Captain Crow entered the Neuro-Link station at a surprisingly slow gait. Instead of walking over to his recliner, he walked directly to the control center where Mackenzie, Tracy Curry, and Crean were located. He had his tablet in his hand and placed it on the console next to Mackenzie as the director began shouting out information at him.

"Crow, we have attacks on both coasts. One in Baltimore, and one in San Diego. The West Coast is the farther of the two destinations, so the military will engage the kaiju in San Diego while you send ROC One—"

Crow cut off the director, "Here. I am sending ROC One *right here*."

Mackenzie looked at Crow, with a puzzled look on his face. "Excuse me, what the hell are you talking about?"

Crow opened his tablet. "I wanted to gather more information in regards to this situation before first talking to Dr. Curry and Dr. Crean, but is seems that Rol-Hama has made his move, and I don't have time to approach the situation with people's feelings in mind." Crow brought up the mangled remains of two burnt and decapitated bodies on his tablet. "Once I knew that Rol-Hama was capturing cryptids, growing them to enormous heights, and then on some level exerting enough control over them to attack a city, the thought occurred to me that outside of Curry and Crean there was probably a short list of scientists who could have helped Rol-Hama achieve what he has with the cryptids. The list was roughly four to five people deep of scientists who may have been able to enlarge a living thing to kaiju size. The list of people who could somehow control those monsters was about two to three people deep. Not surprisingly, all of the people on this list had worked with Curry or Crean at one point in their careers. Of the people on that list only two are not currently accounted for."

He pointed to the two bodies. "Fifteen months ago, on the exact same day, one Dr. Harold Teig and Martian Branson were killed in separate car accidents where their bodies were decapitated and their heads and hands were burnt or smashed beyond the ability to

ID them. They were in their cars, and because of that, it was ruled that both bodies were indeed Teig and Branson."

Both Curry and Crean gasped when they heard the names.

Out of respect, Crow waited a second before continuing, "Teig and Branson also happen to have been collegiate professors for both Curry and Crean."

Crow brought up a picture of Rol-Hama. "This is not just the face of madman. It's the face of a strategic genius. No one would even notice if two men who were not connected in any way died in separate states, in grisly accidents on the same day. Statistically it happens every day. The fact that neither victim was able to be identified by the remains could also be overlooked since they were both reported to have left in their cars the morning that they died." Crow took a deep breath. "I am sure that Rol-Hama staged these men's deaths and that he captured them and forced them to enlarge the cryptids and control them." Crow brought up the addresses for both men. "I am also guessing that if you were to check on these men's families that you will find that they are under Thuggee surveillance. Threatening a person's loved ones is the most effective way to get someone to do what you want."

Crow looked toward Curry and Crean. "If I was able to figure this out you can bet that Rol-Hama was able to piece together that the people who created the ROCs and figured out how to control them must have been associated with Teig and Branson. Tracy Curry and Jillian Crean would have been conspicuous by their absence in any search of Teig and Branson's top students. If I were Rol-Hama, I would have tracked the movements of Curry and Crean's families, and in doing so, I would have found that both of their families were flown into areas near here around the holidays."

Crow looked directly into Mackenzie's eyes. "This blitzkrieg attack of monsters is a diversion. By now Rol-Hama has probably figured out that we can't have many more than four ROCs. He is probably hoping to not only capture Curry and Crean, but also the means to control the ROCs as well. He is using a classic *divided and conquer* attack."

Tracy Curry placed her hand on Crow's shoulder. "Rol-Hama isn't the only strategic genius, is he?"

Mackenzie yelled at Crow, "How do you think that I am going to explain to the President that we just let Baltimore and San Diego be destroyed by giant monsters?"

Crow shrugged. "You won't have to when another monster attacks the Nest in the next hour. You were already planning to have the military deal with the Sasquatch, just have them deal with the Lizard Man as well. In the end, it will be easier to sell than losing the Nest and all four ROCs because you ignored the advice of your senior pilot."

Mackenzie was fuming at the thought that a mere fighter pilot would try and overrule the Director of the CIA. He was about to lay into Crow when the windows of the Nest suddenly turned blood red.

No one was sure what exactly was happening until one of the ground crew came running in from outside and up to Mackenzie. "Sir, there's something horrible outside. It looks like a giant with a moth head, wings, and horrible glowing red eyes!"

Mackenzie turned to Crow, who was already running over to his recliner. "The Mothman! It will take ROC One roughly fifteen minutes to get here from its current position. Get that big bird in the air and over here as quickly as possible. You can tell me how you were right later, but right now, we need you and ROC One to take out that oversized insect."

Crow pulled his neuro-link visor over his head and saw through the eyes of ROC 1. The winged kaiju quickly took to the upper atmosphere where it accelerated to Mach 3 in under thirty seconds. As he was approaching the Nest, the information on the Mothman appeared through his neuro-link:

Mothman– A flying insect-like creature located in Point Pleasant, West Virginia.

Descriptions – He is described as a large white flying creature with moth-like wings and glowing red eyes.

Current data from attack- The creature is currently attacking the Nest. It is 250 feet tall and flying.

CHAPTER 16

The entire building shook. Chunks of ceiling fell to the ground as the Mothman slammed into the Nest. Crow was pushing Roc 1 to fly even faster than it currently was as he silently hoped that the defense force of the base would be able to keep the Mothman occupied long enough for ROC 1 to intervene. There was a loud crack as a large piece of the steel girders from the ceiling of the Nest came crashing down next to Tracy. Crow heard Tracy scream and then he closed his eyes and forced ROC 1 to increase its speed.

The Mothman had a large, powerfully built humanoid body, with the exception that its hands and feet ended in large claws. The beast was a dark gray color except for its burning red eyes, which sent out a powerful light that cascaded the entire compound in an eerie luminance. A group of ten soldiers ran out of the base with their rifles aimed at the kaiju, but when the light from the Mothman's eyes made contact with the soldier's skin, it began to burn their flesh. As the soldiers writhed on the ground, their skin not only burned and blistered, but it began to peel off of their bodies.

One of the terrified soldiers screamed, "Radiation!" Then he ran back inside of the building.

When Mackenzie saw several of the soldiers run back inside with the radiation burns over their bodies, he immediately sent an electronic order throughout the base for all personnel to remain indoors. He cursed, and then looked toward Jillian Crean. "How much longer until ROC One gets here? These buildings were originally built during the Cold War. They can withstand a good amount of radiation, but that creature is going to smash through the roof in a few minutes and there is nothing that we can do to stop it."

Crow was grinding his teeth as he answered for the good doctor, "It's almost here. I can see that dammed bug ahead of ROC One."

Mackenzie shouted, "Move it, Crow! Draw that thing away from here. If the other pilots die then the ROCs will be left without human guides, and then who the hell knows what they'll do?"

Crow didn't answer, he just continued to focus on pushing ROC 1 to its limits as through the monster's eyes he could see the grotesque form of the of the Mothman growing ever larger. ROC 1 was almost upon the massive insectoid, but the Mothman either didn't notice or it did not care that ROC 1 was closing in on it. The monster simply continued to fly around the base bathing it in radiation and slamming its body into the main hangar.

ROC 1 was several hundred feet away from the Mothman when Crow directed the monster to shift its body so that's its claws were extended in front of it. Crow could feel ROC 1 in his head. The monster's instincts were urging Crow to fly above the Mothman and attack the creature's head, but Crow wanted to move the monster from over the top of the building that held Tracy.

As ROC 1 dug his claws into the chest of the Mothman and knocked the monster away from the central hub of the Nest, it occurred to Crow that his first thought was to get the monster away from Tracy. He quickly pushed the thought to the back of his head as ROC 1 drove the Mothman into the ground. Crow directed ROC 1 to start tearing into the monster's face, but the Mothman quickly shifted his gaze upward, and ROC 1 screeched in pain as the radiation from the Mothman's eyes began to burn the cyborg's face. Crow urged ROC 1 to fight through the attack, feeling that by landing one well-placed shot into the Mothman's eyes that he could end the threat of its radioactive vision. For the first time since they had started sharing a neuro-link, ROC 1 was able to resist Crow's command. ROC 1 was slowly starting to move away from the Mothman. Crow was unsure if he was losing control of ROC 1 because of the intense pain that the creature was in or because of interference from the radiation. What he did know was that if ROC 1 simply continued to slowly move away from the Mothman that the giant bird would be cooked to death.

Crow directed ROC 1 to fire a volley of its bladed feathers into the Mothman, and then to take off into the sky. The Mothman screamed in pain and closed his eyes as the diamond coated blades dug into his chest. With the Mothman's eyes closed, ROC 1 was given a brief respite from the cryptid's burning eyes, and the monster had no problem complying with Crow's request to take flight.

ROC 1 soared into the air, and then began streaking away from the Nest. Crow had hoped that the Mothman would chase ROC 1, but as he felt the floor shake beneath his body, he knew that the Mothman was content to let ROC 1 escape so that he could continue to attack the Nest.

Crow cursed, and then directed ROC 1 to turn back around. Once more the idea of saving Tracy went through Crow's mind, and once more he tried to block the thought out. In the spilt second that Crow was thinking about Tracy Curry, ROC 1's instincts again crept in and took control of its body. The gargantuan bird attacked the Mothman in the manner that it had originally wanted to prior to being given an overriding command by Crow. ROC 1 latched its claws onto the Mothman's head using one its long talons to pierce the Mothman's left eye. As the talon embedded itself in the eye socket, the beam of radiation was immediately cut off from the eye, and replaced with a river of blood.

As ROC 1 pulled on the Mothman's head the rest of the monster's body was forced to follow or be decapitated. The Mothman began flapping its wings in the direction that ROC 1 was pulling it in order to keep its head from being ripped off its body. At the speed it was traveling, ROC 1 had made it several miles into the open plains around the Nest before the Mothman was able to direct the gaze of its remaining eye at ROC 1's torso. The radioactive gaze started burning ROC 1's chest, and the avian kaiju was forced to release the insect-like cryptid.

From the outskirts of the fence that surrounded the Nest, two dozen Thuggee cultists watched as the giant bird and the Mothman flew away from the base of the enemy. The Mothman's radioactive eyes had done their job. Most of the base's defense had been disabled by the radioactive stare of the creature. The Thuggee did not know how the eyes of the Mothman worked, but what they did know, was that there was no radioactive fallout from the Mothman's attack. Once the Mothman stopped staring at an individual or area the radiation that was there was simply gone.

During his attack, the Mothman had also disabled the electrical fence and cameras that surrounded the base. The monster's burning gaze had also killed or disabled most of the guards around the complex. Several of the cultists nodded to each other, and then they removed bolt cutters from their backpacks and began cutting into the fence that surrounded the Nest.

The two monsters flew a wide circle away from each other. As ROC 1 circled around, Crow continued to worry that his thoughts about Tracy were allowing ROC 1's instincts to override his commands. Whenever he thought about Tracy Curry and his growing feelings toward her, ROC 1s instincts were able to flow into the monster's movements without Crow's permission. Crow forced all of the feelings that were developing for the young doctor out of his mind. He had survived this long and succeeded in countless missions by being a cold, hard man. With the fate of world hanging in the balance, he quickly convinced himself that now was not the time to start going soft.

Crow commanded ROC 1 to turn around, and as he did, so he saw the Mothman slam into the cybernetic bird. Crow cursed himself for letting his mind be distracted by a woman. He immediately forced his will to subvert the instincts of ROC 1. The Mothman was scratching and clawing at ROC 1, and Crow directed ROC 1 to respond in kind. ROC 1 dug its claws into the Mothman's chest. Next, Crow urged the creature to attack the one eye that was still spewing radiation. The two monsters were a ferocious red blur as they fell to the ground, biting and clawing at each other, while the Mothman continued to assault ROC 1 with radiation.

The interlocked kaiju crashed into the ground sending a cloud of dirt and dust billowing into the air. The Mothman had landed on top of ROC 1, and the cryptid focused his burning stare onto the face of the cyborg while simultaneously using its claws to tear into the bird's body. Crow could almost feel the skin starting to peel away from ROC 1's face. He could also sense that ROC 1's torso was holding the weight of the Mothman with relative ease. That's when the thought occurred to Crow that the Mothman might be more insect than human, which could mean that the monster's body was held together by an exoskeleton rather than an interior bone structure. Crow instructed ROC 1 to stretch its wings out at its side. Once the wings were fully extended, he had ROC 1 bring his wings closing in on either side of the Mothman. ROC 1's diamond coated steel feathers acted like the blades of a giant pair of scissors as they cut the Mothman in half. The torso of the Mothman fell to the left side of ROC 1's body, and the Mothman's legs slumped down across the giant bird. The Mothman's remaining eye blinked for a moment before the pulsating radiation being released from it finally stopped.

ROC 1 stood, and then without making a sound, it began to fly in the direction of California. Crow knew that Baltimore was about twenty minutes closer for ROC 1. He also knew that he needed the time to clear his head about his feelings for Tracy before engaging in a battle with another kaiju.

CHAPTER 17

Saint Petersburg

ROC 3 soared high above the storm clouds which comprised the blizzard that was currently burying St. Petersburg in snow. Sheena Green was in a state of nirvana as ROC 3 flew low over the clouds, and its wings skimmed across the dense condensation. She was enjoying being connected to ROC 3 when she was disturbed by the text that appeared in her line of vision. ROC 3 was confused by the strange symbols that it was seeing, and it took a moment for the conscious part of Green's mind to allow itself enough control of the neuro-link to make sense of the text:

Almas– A bipedal humanoid creature reported to live in the mountains of central Asia.

Descriptions – The Almas is reported to look like a powerfully built Wildman. The Almas is said to have many physical characteristics similar to a Neanderthal.

Current data from attack- The creature has attacked Saint Petersburg in the middle of a blizzard. Information is limited, but the creature has destroyed several blocks and it is reported to be heading for the center of the city. The creature is reported to weigh over 6,000 tons.

After circling around the city several times above the storm, ROC 3 dove through the clouds and into the city itself. The blizzard pelted ROC 3, and the snow quickly started to accumulate on its wings. Even the powerful body of ROC 3 found it difficult to fly through the unrelenting deluge of snow. ROC 3's mind focused on the enemy that it had been sent to destroy. Green had let ROC 3 assume total control of the neuro-link. She had let herself *go* in ROC 3, and she was unwilling to questions the monster's willingness to battle another kaiju head-on in such unfavorable conditions.

As it flew around the city, ROC 3 could see that about half of it was already in ruins. The blood of dead bodies had painted the snow like graffiti on a wall. With the blizzard trapping people in their homes, there was no way that they could evacuate from the Almas' attack. ROC 3 could see the bodies of entire families huddled together as the giant Neanderthal smashed through buildings causing the families' own homes to crush them to death. ROC 3 focused its vision, and it could see the robust body of the Almas ahead of it. The giant was crossing a snow covered intersection as it made its way to attack another building. ROC 3 dropped in altitude so that its body was mere feet above the tops of the buildings of St. Petersburg. ROC 3 screeched a challenge at the Almas and simultaneously back in the Nest, Sheena Green did the same.

The Almas turned around to see the colossal bird just before ROC 3 crashed into its chest. The giant Neanderthal slid backward on the snow covered ground and crashed into the building that it was heading for. ROC 3 could see the bodies of dozens of people falling out of the crushed building, but the kaiju was unconcerned about the deaths of the people of Saint Petersburg. Back in the Nest, Tracy Curry pleaded to Green that she needed to remember the people that she was trying to protect, while simultaneously Mackenzie was typing a message across the neuro-link for Green to watch out for collateral damage. Tracy's words fell on deaf ears, and Mackenzie's message was seen as nothing more than an annoyance to ROC 3, who had no concept of what words were.

Deep with the recesses of the neuro-link, Green knew what the message meant, but she ignored it. She had given herself over to ROC 3. She felt that she had become part of a god and nothing would remove her from her connection to the god again.

ROC 3 fought through the falling snow to circle back around toward the Almas, who had managed to stand up in the remains of the building that it had destroyed. The gargantuan beast picked up a large piece of debris and hurled it at the approaching ROC 3. In most weather conditions, ROC 3 would have easily been able to avoid the projectile, but the blizzard was limiting the kaiju's maneuverability. Over five tons of concrete and steel struck ROC 3 in its right wing. The impact caused the kaiju to lose control of its flight pattern, and it brought ROC 3 sliding across the frozen streets directly in front of the Almas. The robust humanoid lifted his right foot and brought it down onto the neck or ROC 3. The

Almas continued to stomp on ROC 3 until the bird was able to lift its beak off the ground and drive it through the monster's left foot. The Almas howled in pain and as he stepped backward, slipped on the thick snow, and fell onto its back.

ROC 3 slowly rose to its feet where it tried to take to the air once again, but with the blizzard pelting ROC 3, and the buildings of the city blocking the wind, the cyborg was unable to fly. The words *"Climb a building and use it get back into the air!"* Suddenly appeared in ROC 3's line of sight, but as before, the kaiju had no concept of the symbols that it saw.

Tracy was next to Green, pleading with her to assume control of the battle before ROC 3 was killed, but the pilot's conscious mind was beyond the reach of her friend.

ROC 3 continued to operate on its own instincts. The kaiju slowly walked over to the fallen Almas, and then it climbed on top of the creature and began using its beak to attack the monster's round face. ROC 3 struck the Almas in the face several times, creating deep cuts, and slicing open one of its eyes.

The Almas struck ROC 3 with its club like hand, sending the massive bird tumbling across the snow covered street. The mighty bird skidded to a stop, and then it looked up to see the Almas lumbering toward it. ROC 3 screeched once more, stood, and then began slowly walking toward the creature to re-engage it in battle.

Back in the Nest, Mackenzie cursed, "What in the hell is Green doing? She isn't using any of her long range weapons or taking advantage of her speed and agility in the air!"

Tracy was checking the neuro-link feed on the computer. "Green isn't giving any input into the neuro-link. ROC Three is controlling all of its own movements, and its acting like a kaiju. It's just attacking in attempt to destroy its enemy."

Mackenzie's face turned pale. "Do you mean that ROC Three has subverted Green's consciousness?"

Tracy shook her head. "No. Green if fully capable of directing the movements of ROC Three, they are in perfect sync. It's more like Green has simply opted to let her consciousness drift into that of ROC Three." She glared at Mackenzie. "This is what happens when you let a mentally unstable person engage in a neuro-link with a kaiju."

The Almas and ROC 3 met in the middle of Saint Petersburg, and there was primordial hatred between the two them. The Neanderthal ancestors of the Almas and the dinosaur bird hybrids from which the ROCs were derived were natural enemies of each other. Each species viewed the other as a food source. The two kaiju roared at each other as the blizzard continued to increase in intensity.

ROC 3 struck first, slashing the Almas across the chest with the bladed feathers of its wings. A long gash opened on the Almas' chest, and blood spurted out of it spraying ROC 3.

The Almas brought his right fist crashing into ROC 3's chest.

The cybernetic kaiju slid backward on the ice and fell onto its back.

The Almas sprung on top of its enemy and began using its massive fists to pound on ROC 3.

The wild man was too heavy for ROC 3 to move off its chest. ROC 3 screeched in pain as the bones it its ribcage and right wing shattered under the assault of the Almas.

Mackenzie was frantically typing in suggestions to Green that continued to go unheeded.

Tracy's blood ran cold as she heard Green screech in pain, just like ROC 3. She left her computer and ran over to Green in order to make one last attempt to help her friend. She grabbed the neuro-link display that was over Green face. Tracy was going to tear the helmet off Green and break the neuro-link with the kaiju before ROC 3 died from the assault of the Almas.

The helmet was halfway off Green's head, and it was only losing her connection to ROC 3 that forced her consciousness to resume control of the link. She pulled her helmet back over her head, and screamed, "No! We are one and the same. If ROC 3 dies, then so do I! I can't live without it."

Green pushed Tracy to the ground, and then she forced her mind to resume control of ROC 3. The Almas continued to pound on ROC 3, shattering several more bones, and as Sheena Green resumed control of ROC 3, she knew that the majestic monster would never rise off of the frozen streets of St. Petersburg. Green resolved herself that if ROC 3 was going to die that it would at least take the Almas with it. Green urged ROC 3 to hold on to life as long as possible, waiting for the Almas to move itself into optimal position. Finally, after several more devastating blows, the Almas lifted both of his hands over his head in preparation of crushing ROC 3's skull.

When Green saw the Almas' throat exposed, she forced ROC 3 to swipe its still functioning wing across the man-beast's throat. When the bladed feathers on ROC 3's wing hit their target a river of crimson poured out of the Almas' throat.

The giant grabbed his throat in a vain attempt to try and stop the blood gushing out of it. The Almas stood and stumbled forward several steps before it finally bled out and fell down in the snow face first.

Through ROC 3's eyes, Green watched as the Almas finally died. For the final time, ROC 3 and Sheena Green screeched in unison, and then the mighty ROC 3 died.

Tracy was watching her screen of the neuro-link, and she gasped when she saw the brainwaves of both ROC 3 and Sheena Green flat line.

Mackenzie ran over to the pilot and put his hand on her jaw. "Thank God! I have a pulse, and she is still breathing."

Tracy Curry broke down in tears. "She's alive, but she's brain dead. The sensation of feeling ROC 3 perish through the neuro-link was too much for her mind to handle. Her brain will continue to keep her bodily processes going, but her consciousness will never return." She slumped down in her chair. "Sheena will spend the rest of her life in a vegetative state."

CHAPTER 18

Tracy was still crying when the windows and doors around the central building of the Nest suddenly shattered inward allowing several dozens Thuggee cultists to storm into the building.

Mackenzie pulled a handgun from his belt and shot down two of the approaching cultists. He then looked around the room to see the men who were suffering from radiation burns being shot to pieces by the merciless fanatics. The director quickly realized that this assault could mean the end of their ability to fight off Rol-Hama's cryptids. He fired at another cultist only to have a hail of bullets strike the control panel in front of him. He looked over to see the pilots still engaged in the neuro-links with their ROCs. The cultists did not seem to be attacking the vulnerable pilots, and Mackenzie guessed that the cultists were simply unaware that it was the incapacitated people in recliners who were controlling the ROCs. Three more armed guards ran into the room and joined Mackenzie under his control console. He yelled out directions to the men, "We have to try and protect the pilots without giving away to the Thuggee how vital they are to our operation!"

The guards nodded that they understood, and then the four men broke off from their position and began to fire at the cultists that quickly surrounded them.

A hail of bullets sprayed around Tracy Curry and Jillian Crean.

Jillian had been helping some of the guards who had suffered radiation burns, while at the same time continuing to watch the information on the physical status of the remaining ROCs, and doing what she could to fight off the invaders. When the invasion had started she grabbed one of the soldier's guns and began firing at the cultists.

Tracy had another idea in mind about how to help. She knew that she could do little in battle, but she also knew that they had one of the most dangerous weapons on the planet at their disposal. All that Tracy needed to do was to activate that weapon. Bullets sailed over Tracy's head as she crawled on her stomach toward Tobias Crow.

Mackenzie fired the last two bullets from his handgun. He had managed to kill two more of the cultists, but he was now out of ammunition. His problem was solved when the guard who was next to him was shot in the head and fell to the ground. He grabbed the guard's rifle and continued to fire back at the cultists. Mackenzie took a moment to see how the battle was playing itself out. Despite Tracy Curry and Jillian Crean being in relatively unprotected spots, they were not being fired upon. Mackenzie quickly surmised that the only reason they were not being fired upon was because the cultists were there to abduct the two scientists.

Tracy finally reached Crow. She yanked his neuro-link headset off knowing that ROC 1 would continue the last command that Crow had given it, which was to fly to California.

Crow snapped awake and immediately sprang into action. He pulled his handgun and knife from his belt, and then rolled toward the wall of the complex. When he reached the wall he sprang up and began firing at cultists. He quickly dropped five of them to the ground.

Tracy watched in disbelief at how quickly the man moved. After firing off several shots, he seemed to fade into the shadows of the building.

A cultist had taken up a position near a window that he smashed through and was firing on Mackenzie's position. The cultist was preparing to reload his weapon when Crow's arm shot out from the shadows and wrapped around the man. A second later Crow slit the man's throat.

The cultist next to the man Crow had killed turned to fire on Crow, but before he could do so, Crow lunged at him and buried his knife in the cultist's heart. Crow immediately pulled the knife from the man's chest and threw it another cultist. The knife struck the man between the eyes, and he fell to the ground with the knife still sticking out of his head.

Crow picked up the automatic weapon that the man had dropped and quickly gunned down four more members of the Thuggee. Crow's carnage caused the remaining cultists to focus their attention on him. A hail of bullets exploded around Crow, and he was forced to jump behind the cover of the steel beam that served as one of the supports for the building. Bullets clanged off the steel support as Crow waited for an opportunity to attack again. In his mind, he was at least glad that the cultists were firing upon him and not at his fellow pilots or Tracy.

With Crow's attack drawing the attention of the remaining cultists, Mackenzie, the remaining guards, and even Jillian Crean sprang into action, and they gunned down all but two of the cultists. The remaining cultists attempted to flee, but Crow shot each of them in the knees, causing them to fall to the ground.

One of the cultists punched himself in the face and screamed out the names of Rol-Hama and Kali. A second later his mouth filled with foam as the cyanide pill embed in his tooth ended his life.

As Crow was moving toward the fallen cultists, he removed his knife from the head of the man he had thrown in into. The one remaining cultist was about to punch himself in the face when Crow tossed his knife and impaled it in the man's arm. The cultist screamed in pain and grabbed the knife that was buried in his wrist. Crow jumped on the man then pulled his knife out of the man's arm. With a swipe of his blade, Crow cut out a section of the cultist's lower jaw to prevent him from accessing the pill drilled into his tooth. The cultist was screaming in pain as Crow yelled, "I know that Rol-Hama is in the tribal region of Pakistan. I saw the spider in his bunker. It is only found in that area of Pakistan. Save us time and yourself a lot of pain by giving me his exact location."

The cultist shook his head in defiance of Crow's request."

Mackenzie, the guards, Crean, and Tracy had come running over to Crow and his captive.

Mackenzie stood next to Crow. "Tells us where he is or we will make you tell us!"

Once more the man shook his head no.

Crow looked at Tracy, he then grabbed the man by the throat and drug him to the corner. All that Tracy could hear Crow say as he dragged the man to the shadows was, "Let me give you one piece of advice." Crow spoke to the man quietly, the man quickly mumbled some coordinates, and then Crow struck him over the head with the butt of his knife—rendering the cultist unconscious.

Crow walked back over to Mackenzie. "I have the location of Rol-Hama." Crow gave the coordinates to Mackenzie, and then he walked back to his recliner to re-engage in the neuro-link with ROC 1.

Once Crow was back in the neuro-link, Tracy walked over to Mackenzie. "What did Crow say to that man that made him give up Rol-Hama so quickly?"

Mackenzie shook his head. "Trust me, you don't want to know."

Tracy nodded in reply, and then she saw to having Sheena Green moved to the medical bay.

CHAPTER 19

Sydney

ROC 4 was in flight heading toward Sydney. Bixby's mind was still on Munroe and his feelings for her, but rather than cause him distress, his feelings for Munroe actually seemed to calm him as he engaged in the neuro-link with ROC 4. Having sex with Munroe was one thing, but the prospect of having a meaningful relationship with someone was an experience that Bixby never thought that he would enjoy. He had not yet found the right time to talk about these newly discovered feelings with Munroe. He hoped that she at least had inklings of feelings toward him. Regardless of her feelings toward him, he had a mission, and as the information on the crypitd that he pursued came across his neuro-link, he focused on what he needed to do.

Flying Rod– Cylindrical shaped cryptid often with a fin or sail that runs along its body.

Descriptions – Flying Rods are cryptids which move at speeds beyond the ability of the human eye to see. These creatures can only be seen in pictures and on film. The Rods fly at incredible speeds, and some cryptozoologists suggest that the Rods may be interdimensional beings.

Current data from attack– There is only one known picture of the Rod that is currently attacking Sydney. The Rod appears to have a length of over 1,000 feet and it is roughly 30 feet thick. The creature's weight is unable to be determined. What is known is that the creature is able to fly at speeds and complete aerial maneuvers far beyond the capabilities of the ROCs or any other known method of flight.

The information was as almost as confusing to Bixby as were his thoughts on how to express his feelings to Munroe. The creature that he was after was a giant flying rod with fin-like appendages around it, and it may or may not be an interdimensional being that was unable to be seen by the human eye! This unorthodox creature was reported to move at speeds well beyond the speed of sound without breaking the sound barrier. Bixby felt like yelling back at the information that Mackenzie had sent him, *"How am even supposed to engage a creature that may or may not be corporeal?"*

As ROC 4 flew over Sydney, Bixby was astounded at the level of devastation that the Rod had already caused in the city. More than two thirds of the city was rubble or dust. Tens of thousands of people were lying dead across the streets. Bixby saw a building to the right of ROC 4 suddenly explode outward, but he was unable to perceive anything that could have caused the destruction. To his left, another building exploded, sending debris and bodies hurtling into the streets. Bixby directed ROC 4 to fly in the direction of the explosion, and as ROC 4 swerved in the air, it was suddenly struck in its left side. ROC 4 swerved to regain control of its flight path, but it had no sooner righted itself than it was struck on the back half of its body. The blow caused ROC 4 to spin in a circle in midair, and then crash to the ground. ROC 4 righted itself and it attempted to find its attacker only to be struck in the face with a force comparable to a freight train running into it at full speed.

ROC 4 stumbled backward. Bixby realized that he had to change his tactics quickly or else ROC 4 was not going to last long. For a brief moment, he feared for his own mortality, and he thought of Munroe and of a future with her. In the moment that he thought of Munroe, he caught a glimpse of something approaching ROC 4 from the right, and instinctively, the giant bird ducked its head. Bixby directed ROC 4 to turn its head in the direction of the object that had just shot passed, but as ROC 4 turned its head, he could see nothing but the ruins of Sydney.

ROC 4 was still looking for its attacker when something slammed into its midsection and knocked the giant bird onto its back. As ROC 4 was knocked down Bixby's thoughts once more quickly drifted to Munroe, and it was in that instant that he saw a long, thick body with undulating fins fly over ROC 4. Bixby smiled to himself as he realized what was going on. Whenever he thought about Munroe and a possible future with her, he become more in touch with his feelings to connect with someone else. When he accessed these feelings it helped him to form a stronger neuro-link with ROC 4. With a stronger neuro-link, he was able to see the Rod through ROC 4's eyes, and then process it with his superior mind. Bixby closed his eyes, and then for a brief moment, pictured himself and Munroe walking hand and hand on beach after they had ended this war with Rol-Hama and his cryptid kaiju.

He opened his eyes to see the huge Rod streaking toward ROC 4. Bixby let ROC 4's reflexes react to the attack while he processed how to counter-attack the fast moving cryptid. ROC 4 took to the sky as Bixby thought about how to attack an object that moved much faster than even ROC 4 was able to, while at the same time keeping the pleasant picture of himself and Munroe on the beach in the back of mind.

Back at the Nest, still distraught, Tracy Curry watched in amazement as Bixby's and ROC 4's brain patterns started moving almost in unison. She noticed that the two thought patterns were not overlapping and becoming one stream of consciousness, as did Green and ROC 3, but rather they working together to improve the functions of each other. Tracy smiled to herself. Whatever Bixby was doing, he had almost figured out how to create an optimal sync with his ROC. She made a mental note to talk to Bixby about his experience after his mission was complete. Perhaps what Bixby had discovered could prevent another pilot from sharing the same fate of Sheena Green and ROC 3.

ROC 4 was soaring over the skies of Sydney when the Rod slammed into its tail. ROC 4 tumbled several thousand feet before steadying itself and regaining altitude. ROC 4 had risen to nearly five thousand feet when it saw the Rod streaking ahead of it from below. Bixby attempted to have ROC 4 fire several of its bladed wings in front of the Rod. He had hoped to hit the Rod as an NFL quarterback would hit a wide receiver in stride by leading with the pass, but the Rod moved even faster than the speed of the falling blades, and the projectiles missed their target by several hundred feet.

ROC 4 watched as the Rod circled around so that it was directly beneath the giant bird, and then it streaked straight up. ROC 4 titled its body to the left so that the Rod clipped its midsection rather than hitting it head-on but even a glancing blow from something moving that fast still caused some damage. ROC 4 tumbled over twice before again regaining control of its flight pattern. ROC 4 had enough time to look up and see the Rod diving for it again. This time ROC 4 was unable to roll with the blow, and the massive Rod hit ROC 4 squarely in the back. The kaiju was being driven into the ground at a speed beyond belief. As Bixby saw the ground quickly getting closer he doubted that even ROC 4 could survive from slamming into the earth at such a velocity. It was then that Bixby's high school physics classes kicked in. He knew that force the Rod was hitting ROC 4 with was caused by its mass moving at such a high velocity. Bixby knew that while some people claimed that the Rod was an interdimensional being he hoped that it still had to adhere to the laws of basic physics.

Bixby directed ROC 4 to fold it wings alongside its body, dip its body down, and at the same time unleash a blast of the liquid nitrogen stored in its neck. As ROC 4 completed the maneuver the Rod slid off its back and was immediately frozen solid by the liquid nitrogen. ROC 4 once more steadied itself in the air, and Bixby watched as the thick coating of frost on the Rod shattered, freeing it from the effects of the liquid nitrogen. The Rod had freed itself from its icy coating but it was unable to stop its descent as it slammed into the ground and caused a large crater to form.

Bixby was unsure if the crash had destroyed the Rod, but just in case it didn't, he urged ROC 4 to start gaining altitude and speed. ROC 4 looked down to see the Rod flying out of the crater that it had created. ROC 4 passed Mach 5, and seconds later, Mach 6, but the Rod was still gaining on the kaiju by the millisecond. Bixby knew that in order for his plan to work his thought process would have to work in perfect harmony with ROC 4's reflexes, because otherwise, this was probably be the last maneuver that ROC 4 would ever make. Still through the link, Bixby could sense that ROC 4 trusted him, and for the first time, the feeling was totally mutual.

ROC 4 surpassed Mach 7 and it had entered the upper atmosphere where it sprayed another blast of liquid nitrogen in front it before folding its wings and starting a freefall back to Earth.

The Rod shot past ROC 4 missing it by mere feet and running directly into the cloud of liquid nitrogen. The frozen Rod continued to streak higher.

ROC 4 looked up to see the cryptid enter the stratosphere before it was able to shatter the ice that had encased it, but at that point, it was too late. The cryptid had flown so high and so fast that it had escaped Earth's gravity, and it shot out into space.

Bixby smiled, and thought to himself, *simple physics*. An object in motion stays in motion until it is acted on by outside force. When an object is flying in the atmosphere it is able to change course by changing the air flow around it, but in space there is no air or gravity, so changing course requires multiple propulsion systems. Spaceships could not simply fly through space quickly changing course and neither could the Rod. The cryptid continued to streak deeper into space, and it would continue its journey until it accidently was pulled into the gravitational field of a sun, planet, or black hole. Bixby guessed that the Rod would hit one of those things in about several thousand years.

He had ROC 4 maintain a high altitude and speed as he headed for Europe. Munroe was potentially facing two monsters, and there was no way that he was going to let her fight those battles alone.

CHAPTER 20

London

As ROC 2 flew toward the city of London all that Munroe could see were flames. A large portion of the city was burning, and she could see fire brigades doing their best to slow the advance of the inferno from consuming the entire city. The rest of the city was completely dark, and Munroe guessed that the monster attacking city must have taken out part of its power grid. The brigades would stop the fires that were already burning from spreading, but Munroe knew that it was up to her and ROC 2 to stop the fires at their source.

The information on her target was sketchy for several reasons. The monster that she was going to face had not been seen regularly for several centuries.

Spring Heeled Jack – a humanoid with a demonic appearance known for attacking people in Victorian England. The creature was said to breathe fire and to be able to jump to extreme heights

Descriptions – He was described as having a terrifying appearance, wearing a long cloak, with metal clawed hands. Speculation on the origins of Jack ranged from a few people in elaborate costumes to the spawn of Hell itself.

Current data from attack- Spring Heeled Jack is reported to be roughly 150 feet tall and weighs roughly 2,000 tons. The creature has a humanoid body, and he is wearing a long black cloak and slacks. He has a hunched over appearance, and he is walking around with his knees bent in a crouched position. Jack has clawed metal hands that have been tearing through buildings, and he is confirmed to be able to project blasts of blue flames from his mouth.

ROC 2 circled the city as Munroe took in the information. This creature was relatively small by the standards of other monsters the ROCs had faced. ROC 2 was nearly twice the size of Jack. Munroe was thinking about how to approach a smaller opponent as

ROC 2 continued to fly over the city looking for its target. When a burst of blue flame shot up from the area known as Piccadilly Circus, ROC 2 zeroed in on the area, and the cyborg flew straight for it.

ROC 2 was flying toward Piccadilly Circus when it was surprised as a hellish looking creature suddenly appeared in front of it in mid-air. The malevolent creature first slashed ROC 2 across the face, and then it spit a burst of blue flames onto the winged kaiju. ROC 2 veered away from the attack, with the blue flames still flickering on its feathers, as Jack fell back to the city streets below.

Back in her recliner, Munroe squirmed as she could actually feel the flames singe the inside of her body. Munroe was taken aback by the fact that she felt the attack herself through the neuro-link. She quickly reviewed the information on Jack and zeroed in on the theory that Jack was a Hell spawned creature. She briefly wondered if the fire the monster spewed was actuality Hellfire. Munroe was not one for metaphysical speculation, and she quickly refocused on the task at hand. Even if Munroe's very soul was being burned she had a monster to kill and lives to save, and she was determined to be successful in her mission.

ROC 2 circled around and flew low over the city, but the kaiju was unable to locate the demonic monster. At only one hundred and fifty meters tall, Jack was roughly the same size as the majority of the buildings that surrounded him. With Jack wearing a dark cloak and the city plunged into blackout, even ROC 2's enhanced vision was having difficulty spotting the monster.

The winged kaiju was flying slowly over the skyline when Jack leapt out from behind a building and covered the upper half of ROC 2 in flames. Both ROC 2 and Munroe's bodies were racked with pain from the flames. ROC 2 gained altitude and fired a volley of its bladed feathers at Jack, but the agile beast was able to leap clear of the blades, and he once more hid in the shadows of the city's buildings. Munroe realized that she needed to change her method of engaging Jack.

Jack had purposely set up the city to benefit him in a battle. He could strike and retreat into the darkness before ROC 2 had the chance to respond. Munroe began thinking of how Bixby would bust her balls about how the relatively small Jack had defeated

ROC 2. As she was thinking about Bixby, she suddenly experienced a new sensation through the neuro-link with ROC 2. ROC 2 had the largest naval cavity of any creature that had ever lived, and Jack had the distinct smell of brimstone about him. Jack could hide from ROC 2's eyes in the darkness with his cloak, but he could not hide his horrible stench from ROC 2's olfactory senses.

Munroe had ROC 2 take a deep breath of air, and the kaiju immediately sensed where its prey was. Now that Munroe was able to locate Jack, she also had a plan for how to defeat the demon. ROC 2 landed on a large building that Jack was hiding next to.

As ROC 2 landed, Jack threw off the black cloak that blended him into the city streets, and unleashed a blast of Hellfire at ROC 2. Anticipating Jack's attack, Munroe had ROC 2 spew a cloud of liquid nitrogen at the cryptid. When the wave of Hellfire met the mist of sub-zero chemicals, the two opposing forces caused a cloud to form with long arcs of static electricity escaping from it. ROC 2 used the cloud to fire a volley of its bladed feathers at Jack.

The demonic figure howled in pain as the blades embedded themselves in his chest and legs. Jack leapt around the nearest corner, and then he zigzagged through several more streets in an attempt to hide himself.

ROC 2 took another whiff of air, and it was immediately able to locate the beast. ROC 2 flew high in the direction of the foul odor of brimstone. As ROC 2 closed in on Jack, it fired another set of bladed feathers at the creature. Most of the blades missed, but the volley kept Jack from leaping into the air at ROC 2, and it also forced Jack to move in the direction of the Thames River. Munroe instructed ROC 2 to continue to use its sense of smell to keep track of Jack and to use it bladed feather attack to steer the cryptid closer to river.

After several minutes of leaping from street to street in an attempt to avoid the piercing blades of ROC 2, Spring Heeled Jack found himself on the banks of the Thames River. Jack turned around from the water's edge to see ROC 2 bearing down on him. Jack reared back and spewed a blast of Hellfire at the kaiju.

ROC 2 shifted the front end of its body upward, and then it began to flap its wings in rapid succession. The action caused a wall of wind to collide with the blast of Hellfire, and it caused the blast to fold back onto itself and return to its starting point.

Jack screeched in pain and fear as his own blue flames engulfed his body. Jack's cloak was still burning when he looked up to see ROC 2 flying toward him with its talons extended.

ROC 2 sank its talons into Jack's torso and through his back. ROC 2 then lifted Jack into the air and brought him crashing down into the river. Jack looked up through the cold, murky waters of the Thames to see the beak of ROC 2 bearing down on him. Jack tried to blast the kaiju with his Hellfire, but the river immediately doused his flames and filled the demons lungs with water.

ROC 2's beak plunged through the surface of the river and latched onto Jack's head. With her talons holding the demon firmly beneath her and her beak crushing Jack's skull, ROC 2 pulled and ripped Spring Heeled Jack's head off his shoulders.

Munroe could sense that ROC 2 was hungry, and they still had to fight the Loch Ness Monster in an attempt to save what was left of Glasgow. She disconnecting herself from the neuro-link as ROC 2 fed upon the corpse of Spring Heeled Jack. The experience of ROC 2 devouring that horror was not something Munroe wished to share. As her mind readjusted to her surroundings in the Nest, she was shocked to see the carnage that had occurred there. When Munroe was in a neuro-link it was difficult for her senses to process what was occurring around her body. Munroe had the vague sense that there was some kind commotion occurring in the Nest, but she had no idea that a full scale shootout had occurred. She looked across from her station to see that Green was not in her recliner. Munroe's heart skipped a beat as she thought about Bixby. Her head snapped to the left to see Bixby sitting safely in his recliner, and a wave of relief washed over her. Bixby was smiling like a school boy as he guided ROC 4 to his next mission. For the first time since she had met him, Munroe thought that Bixby looked cute. She had always thought that he was hot, but this was the first time that she saw him as more than a friend with benefits.

She pushed her feelings for Bixby aside and the questions that she had about the battle which had occurred in the Nest would have to wait. Two minutes had passed, and she needed to re-engage in the neuro-link with ROC 2. When she re-engaged in the link, Munroe was thankful that ROC 2 had finished its grisly meal. Munroe directed ROC 2 to take the air, and then she had the kaiju headed north to Scotland at top speed.

CHAPTER 21

ROC 1 streaked toward San Diego at Mach 6. Between ROC 1's fight with the Mothman, his realization of his feelings for Tracy Curry, and the attack on the Nest, Tobias Crow was extremely emotionally charged. He was looking forward to letting loose some of those emotions on the giant Sasquatch tearing apart San Diego. Crow had some idea that his emotional state was interfering with ROC 1's thought process. In truth, Crow's emotions were overwhelming ROC 1 and suppressing the kaiju's natural reflexes and instincts.

With guards suffering from radiation burns and dead bodies all across the complex, Tracy Curry was busy doing what she could to get the injured to the medical facility. If the young doctor was not so preoccupied with everything that was going on around her, she would have noticed that ROC 1's neuro-link was almost non-existent. Sheena Green had let herself be lost in ROC 3's mind, but Crow was using his singular determination to subdue ROC 1's consciousness.

Crow was almost at San Diego when Mackenzie was finally able to send the information on the Sasquatch through his neuro-link display:

Sasquatch (Bigfoot)– Massive bipedal ape-like creature.

Descriptions – The Sasquatch are large primates that are covered in hair and have extremely long arms and legs with a powerful body.

Current data from attack- The Sasquatch that is attacking San Diego stands at 330 feet tall and weighs just under 6,000 tons. The creature has proven itself to be extremely powerful and durable. High powered guns and missiles have been unable to hurt the creature. The creature is reported to be extremely physically powerful and agile.

Crow read the information and internalized it. He was ready for a challenge, and it seemed as if this Sasquatch would be the most powerful cryptid that the ROCs had yet to face. Crow had ROC 1 fly low as it entered the city. Locating the Sasquatch was not difficult. The kaiju was tearing apart the business district as if the buildings were made of matchsticks.

The Sasquatch looked directly at ROC 1 as the giant bird streaked toward him. The cryptid snarled, tore the top of a building from its foundation, then hurled it at ROC 1.

Crow had ROC 1 swerve to the side, but with ROC 1's reflexes being suppressed by Crow's strong will, the winged kaiju did not react quickly enough and the building clipped its left wing. ROC 1 came crashing down into a set of buildings that quickly collapsed around the kaiju. Crow commanded ROC 1 to stand, and when he did, Crow saw the Sasquatch charging at ROC 1 at a speed that belied the creature's size and weight. Crow had ROC 1 open his wings and fire a barrage of bladed feathers at the charging cryptid. The blades dug deep into the Sasquatch's skin, but the attack did not slow the gargantuan creature in the least. ROC 1 had started to ascend into the sky just as the Sasquatch was upon it. The Sasquatch grabbed ROC 1 by its wings, and the cryptid attempted to rip the appendages off of the cyborg.

Crow had ROC 1 use it curved beak to begin striking the Sasquatch in the face. The first strike caught the Sasquatch off guard, but the monster ignored the second and third strike as it continued to apply unbelievable pressure to ROC 1's wings. Crow was sure that ROC 1 was going to be torn in half any second, and he ordered ROC 1 to unleash a blast of liquid nitrogen into the Sasquatch's face. As the freezing chemical hit the Sasquatch in his eyes, mouth, and nose, the monster released its hold on ROC 1, allowing the majestic bird to ascend into the sky.

The Sasquatch grabbed its face and roared as ROC 1 circled overhead. ROC 1 flew in a straight line away from the monster, and then Crow had the cyborg turn around. The Sasquatch's back was to ROC 1 as the massive bird approached the monster at a speed just below the sound barrier. ROC 1 slammed into the Sasquatch with enough force to plow through a city block, and while the beast stumbled forward a few steps, it did not fall. Crow was astounded at the monster's strength. For the first time, he wondered if ROC 1 was going to fail in its mission.

Crow had ROC 1 send another volley of bladed feathers into the back of the Sasquatch, and with a speed quicker than Crow could react to, the monster spun around and delivered a crushing blow to the chest of ROC 1. ROC 1 was sent tumbling down the street tearing apart buildings, cars, and power lines in its wake. When ROC 1 stopped stumbling it lifted its head to see the Sasquatch sprinting down the street. Crow urged ROC 1 to stand and start spewing liquid nitrogen at the charging cryptid. ROC 1 complied with the command, and the Sasquatch ran directly into a cloud of sub-zero mist. The monster reached through the freezing mist and grabbed ROC 1 by its right wing. It was only the thin layer of ice on the Sasquatch's hand that allowed ROC 1 to slip out of the monster's grip. ROC 1 began flapping its wings, causing it to rise into the sky. Crow could feel ROC 1's flight or fight response urging him to flee from this creature.

Crow countermanded ROC 1's impulses, and thought to himself, *I thought you were a ROC not a chicken!*

Crow had ROC 1 several hundred feet above the Sasquatch, and then he directed ROC 1 to begin firing all of its remaining bladed feathers at the cryptid. The blades dug deep into the flesh of the monster, but despite his skin being sliced to pieces, the Sasquatch jumped up, and to the surprise of Crow and ROC 1, he grabbed ROC 1 by the talon. As the Sasquatch was falling back to Earth, he pulled on ROC 1's talon and added his tremendous strength to the momentum of his fall.

ROC 1 crashed through the city streets and into the subway system below. Crow immediately knew that the impact had broken ROC 1 wings. The mighty kaiju was helpless as the Sasquatch looked down at his injured adversary and roared. As Crow saw the ominous hand of the Sasquatch reaching down to grab ROC 1, he tore the neuro-link headpiece off of his head. Crow knew what had happened to Green when she refused to leave her ROC as it died, and Crow had no desire to live the rest of his life in a coma.

Mackenzie turned his face to Crow with a look of concern. "What happened?"

Crow shook his head. "We are about to lose ROC 1. That Sasquatch is the most powerful thing that I have ever seen."

Back in San Diego, the Sasquatch wrapped his hand around the head of ROC 1 forcing the bird's beak closed. The cryptid then lifted ROC 1 out of the crater it was buried in, and the monster squeezed, crushing the skull of ROC 1. The mighty ROC 1 fell to ground as its grey matter spilled onto the city streets through its shattered head. The Sasquatch stepped on top of his fallen foe and roared in triumph. With his victory complete, the man-beast resumed his goal of turning the city of San Diego into dust.

CHAPTER 22

ROC 2 soared over the moors of England as it made its way north to Scotland. Munroe pushed ROC 2 at close to top speed knowing full well that the Loch Ness Monster already had over an hour of attacking Glasgow. Munroe had pretty much resigned herself to the fact the Glasgow was a lost cause and that she was basically trying to take out the monster before it had the opportunity to attack another city.

She was nearing the borders of Scotland when the information from Mackenzie on the monster flashed across her neuro-link:

Loch Ness Monster (Nessie) – A legendary reptilian cryptid reported to live in Loch Ness.

Description – Various reports portray the creature differently. The similarities in reports include a long reptilian neck and thin body.

Data from Current Attack – Nessie entered Glasgow from the Atlantic Ocean. She has the appearance of a serpent with relatively short arms at the front and rear of her torso. Reported to be roughly 700 feet long and weighing around 6,000 tons. The creature is able to move on land by slithering like a snake, but it has also been reported to be able to rear up on its back legs to attack tall buildings.

The remains of Glasgow came into sight for ROC 2. The city was in ruins, and Munroe didn't even want to think about the number of people who had already died. It looked as only the northern most section of the city was still intact, and Munroe had every intention of keeping it that way.

ROC 2's eyes were fixed on the remaining skyline of the northern part of the city when it saw a large serpentine-like head suddenly looming over the buildings. As Munroe looked through ROC 2's eyes, she was surprised to see a very different monster than what she thought that she would be facing. Every picture that she had seen of Nessie had looked like plesiosaur-type dinosaur, but the creature she now beheld looked like something more akin to a Chinese Dragon rather than an ancient marine reptile. When she saw the monster's head smash through buildings, she realized that the monster's appearance was inconsequential. What did matter was that she and ROC 2 were going to put an end to this monster here and now.

ROC 4 was streaking over France when Bixby was sent information through his neuro-link from Mackenzie:

ROC 1 and ROC 3 are both down. Baltimore is still under attack. You are to change your flight pattern and head to Baltimore in an attempt to intercept the Lizard Man.

Bixby focused his thoughts so that he was saying his words out loud to Mackenzie in the Nest, "Even at top speed I would never make it Baltimore in time to make a difference. The Lizard Man will be long gone by the time I make it there. We can't afford to lose any more ROCs. I am flying to Glasgow to assist Munroe and ROC Two."

More information from Mackenzie scrolled across Bixby's neuro-link:

You are to head to Baltimore and then see if ROC 4 can track the Lizard Man. That is an order!

Bixby shouted out, "We are down two ROCs because you have not had us working as a team. It's our ability to trust in each other and work together that makes us stronger than the enemy. I am not leaving Munroe alone on this one, and if you don't like it, then you can go and find yourself someone else who is ready to pilot ROC Four. Now, send me the information on the creature that ROC Two and Munroe are fighting."

ROC 4 had finished flying over the English Channel, and it was making its way to Scotland when Mackenzie finally sent the information on Nessie through ROC 4's neuro-link.

Nessie was rearing its head up to strike again when ROC 2 swooped in from behind the monster and buried its talons into the monster's long neck. ROC 2 began clawing and biting at the back of Nessie's neck, but the agile monster snapped it body like a whip and sent ROC 2 hurtling off of it. ROC 2 tumbled a few times before regaining control of its flight pattern. Nessie was still reared up as ROC 2 flew toward it and stuck several dozen bladed feathers into the monster's underbelly.

Nessie hissed and dropped to the ground driving the blades below it further into its flesh. The monster then began to slither through the city like a colossal snake. ROC 2 tried to fire more of its bladed feathers at the creature, but Nessie's movements caused a good portion of the feathers to miss the creature.

ROC 2 flew behind the monster in an attempt to land on the back of its neck, and once more, attacked the area that it had damaged in its initial assault. As ROC 2 was closing in on Nessie, the monster lifted its head and whipped it around to face the oncoming ROC. Nessie snapped its jaws at ROC 2, but the nimble bird was able to evade the creature's attack. ROC 2 flew backward from Nessie's jaws, and then it shot forward using its talons to gouge the Loch Ness Monster across the face. ROC 2 was continuing to press its attack when Nessie's tail crashed into it from behind. ROC 2 was knocked from the air, and it went crashing down into the city streets. ROC 2 was face down in the street and stunned from the blow. With lightning-like speed, Nessie wrapped its long body around ROC 2, and then it began to constrict. ROC 2 was being crushed as if it was a dove and Nessie was a python. Munroe was sure that ROC 2 was about to perish when through ROC 2's ears she heard a high pitched sound growing closer.

ROC 4 could see ROC 2 being crushed, and both Bixby and the kaiju immediately increased their speed. ROC 4 flew directly for Nessie's head and it began to bite and claw at the gigantic serpent. Nessie's grip loosened just enough for Munroe to direct ROC 2 to tilt its head downward and spray Nessie with its liquid nitrogen attack. Nessie's thick hide began to freeze and crack, forcing the monster to release its grip. ROC 2 and ROC 4 both shot up into the air and out of Nessie's reach.

The two ROCs circled above the Loch Ness horror and they surveyed the situation below them. One of the drawbacks of flying the ROCs through the neuro-link was that communication between the two pilots was difficult. If the two pilots were sitting next to each other they might be able to pick up a word or two but effective verbal communication was not possible. ROC 4 turned its head to ROC 2, and as the two birds looked at each other, Bixby came to a frightening realization. It was at this moment while piloting a monster bird and fighting the Loch Ness Monster of all things that he would found out how deep his connection with Munroe truly was.

If they knew each other's minds as well as they knew each other bodies then the two of them could coordinate their attacks effortlessly. The part that scared Bixby was that at the end of the mission they would both know how well they were connected to each other without even saying a word.

Munroe and ROC 2 took the lead as ROC 2 soared down at the monster and hit it with a barrage of bladed feathers. As ROC 2 was veering off from its attack, Nessie extend its neck in an attempt to grab the monster bird. When Nessie's neck was extended, ROC 4 dove in and latched onto the cyrptid's extended neck. With Nessie's thick body stretched out, ROC 4 was able dig its talons deep into the monster's flesh. Blood spurted out of Nessie's neck and over ROC 4. As soon as ROC 4 tasted the lake monster's blood it shot back up into the sky and fired several dozen bladed feathers into Nessie. Once more the Loch Ness Monster extended it neck as far as it could, allowing ROC 2 to swoop in and attack the injured neck. The wound on Nessie's neck doubled in size as ROC 2 tore into the monster. Nessie whipped its head around to attack ROC 2 only to close its jaws on a cloud of freezing cold liquid nitrogen mist.

Nessie swung its head from side to side spraying blood over the decimated streets of Glasgow. As Nessie writhed in pain and anger, ROC 4 swooped in and once more attacked the creature's wounded neck. The stream of blood turned into a river as ROC 4 sliced open an artery in the legendary monster. Nessie fell to the ground and attempted to slither its way back to the ocean, but both ROCs fell upon the monster and they slashed and bit at the area behind the monster's head until it perished.

When Nessie's body finally stopped it spasms, the two ROCs screeched in triumph, and then the famished kaiju began feeding on the deceased cryptid.

Back in the Nest, Tracy Curry had finally managed to get back to her computer station, and she was astounded to see that Munroe and Bixby were both in perfect sync with their ROCs. Neither the pilot nor the ROC was dominating the other, both entities were functioning to access the best traits of the other and channel them into accomplishing a goal.

Munroe and Bixby tore off their helmets, not because they felt the desire to escape the sensation of their ROCs feeding on the carcass of the Loch Ness Monster, but because they desired to see each other. The two young pilots sprang up from their chairs and ran to each other. They kissed in the middle of the room. They had kissed a hundred times before, but this kiss was different than the embraces they had exchanged for purely physical pleasure. This kiss was meant so that each person knew what the other meant them. As they pulled away, Bixby looked into Munroe's eyes, and said, "I love you."

She smiled. "I know."

CHAPTER 23

The day after the blitzkrieg-style attack orchestrated by Rol-Hama had come to an end, Mackenzie was briefing the President, key members of his cabinet, Tracy Curry, and Jillian Crean on the aftermath. Mackenzie took a deep breath, turned on the large monitor in his office, and started his briefing, "Just to bring you up to speed, the destruction worldwide is monumental. While the ROCs managed to destroy the monsters that were attacking Sydney, St. Petersburg, Glasgow, and London, large portions of those cities were still reduced to rubble. The city of Glasgow has been reduced to roughly twenty city blocks, while the cities of Baltimore and San Diego were totally decimated. Early estimates are that it will take at least two decades to complete enough construction in the two cities before people can start moving back into them."

Mackenzie moved on to the next part of his briefing, "The toll on the populations of these cities is twofold. Literally hundreds of thousands of people are dead or missing worldwide. There is some comfort for the dead in that their problems are over. For the millions of refugees from these cities, their problems are just beginning. The refugees from Baltimore are heading to Washington, D.C., in hopes of finding food, shelter, and medical care in the nation's capital. On the other side of the country, the refugees from San Diego are heading to Oakland and San Francisco. None of the host cities are prepared to handle the influx of people. People in all three cities are doing what they can to help those in need. Several hotels have opened their doors to the refugees with assurances from FEMA that the cost of housing the refugees would be refunded to them. Although with the destruction issues facing the nation's economy, I don't think that those hotel owners will ever see a nickel of the money that they are putting out."

Mackenzie perked up a little as he gave the next bit of information, "Even with large hotel chains helping out, the number of refugees exceeded what these establishments had available, and so churches, schools, gyms, and in some cases, private homes, did what they could to help those in need. Basically this same scene is playing itself out across the world in the other nations that suffered attacks."

"Up until this point, we have successfully slain nine of the mutated cryptids that Rol-Hama has captured. There are at least two other kaiju sized cryptids that are a direct threat to the United States. The Sasquatch that has destroyed San Jose and San Diego has returned into the woodlands of the Pacific Northwest again. We also do not know the whereabouts of the giant Lizard Man that attacked Baltimore. The last report on the creature had it heading out into the Atlantic Ocean."

Mackenzie moved onto another slide. "While our ROCs have performed extremely well thus far, we have lost two of the kaiju, and one of our pilots." Mackenzie paused for a moment out of respect for Sheena Green before continuing, "We also suffered an attack directly on the Nest. We suffered the loss of several guards, and we have about dozen guards suffering from radiation poisoning as a result of the Mothman's attack. The good news is that between some excellent investigative and interrogative efforts by Captain Crow, we have found the location of Rol-Hama. We have also determined that he has captured two men who were presumed to have perished in separate car accidents. Dr. Harold Teig and Dr. Martian Branson are the two men who Rol-Hama captured and forced them to help both enlarge his captured cryptids to kaiju size and to direct them to attack specific targets. We assumed that Rol-Hama was applying pressure to them, and when we checked on both of their families, we found numerous cameras in their houses which were feeding to an outside source. We tracked these feeds to their sources where we found abandon Thuggee safe houses. It seems that when the cultists failed to the take the Nest that they decided it was no longer worthwhile to maintain the threat over the families of their prisoners."

Mackenzie looked toward the President, as he began to explain his plan for dealing with the current crisis going forward, "I suggest that at this point we bring ROCs Two and Four back to the U.S. We have confirmed that there are two kaiju still within or close to our borders. We have certainly done enough to show the rest of the world that we will support them as much as possible, and no foreign country would blame us for protecting our own people. I suggest that we position ROC Two on the West Coast and ROC Four on the East Coast so that we are ready to repel an attack from either the Sasquatch or the Lizard Man, as well as the dozens of other cryptids that Rol-Hama might still have across the country."

Tracy Curry spoke up, "I believe that splitting up the ROCs would be a mistake. I would suggest that we send both ROCs to the West Coast."

Mackenzie smirked. 'Excuse me, Dr. Curry, I was unaware of your background in military tactics."

Tracy sneered. "We have multiple people here with military expertise, but I am the only expert that we have when it comes to the neuro-links with the ROCs and their pilots. I am telling you that splitting up ROC Two and ROC Four would be a mistake, and I can prove it." Tracy pulled out her tablet and linked it to the display screen. Two sets of data each came up with two pairs of wavy lines on each set of data. Tracy explained to everyone what they were looking at, "This display shows the neuro-links of Captain Munroe and ROC Two and the link between Captain Bixby and ROC Four. As you can see, the lines in each instance are moving together, but they are not moving in perfect sync. This display was from a week ago." Tracy shifted the display to another set of data that showed four lines moving in almost perfect sync. "This is the display of the neuro-links of Bixby and Munroe with their ROCs when they were working together to battle the Loch Ness Monster. As you can see the links are showing two distinct brainwaves in each case moving in almost perfect sync. The better the sync between ROC and pilot, the better they able to combine their best attributes in the reflexes and sensory input from the ROCs and the cognitive abilities of the pilots. Previously, I thought that the strength of the link would be increased with continued exposure to linking with a ROC. This hypothesis was recently proven to be wrong, and it now appears that the strength of a neuro-link with a ROC is based on the pilot's ability to engage in meaningful relationships. More specifically it is increased when the pilot is able to trust and find comfort in other people. The human brain has a built in plasticity. This means that certain areas of the brain improve in how well they work the more that we access them."

Tracy stopped to make sure that sure that everyone was following what she had said. Once she was sure that everyone understood the concept, she moved on, "The increase in the pilots' ability to sync better with their ROCs during their battle with the Loch Ness Monster seems to have a twofold causation. The first factor is that both Munroe and Bixby have recently realized that they have deeper feelings for each other than they had previously realized. As their minds began to accept this idea, it utilized more of the area of their brains which deals with relationship building."

Tracy pulled up two sets of brain scans onto the viewing screen. "The brain scans on the left side of the screen show Munroe's and Bixby's brains when they first entered this program. The scans on the right show a brain scan that I took of them yesterday. As you can see in both pilots, the upper left quadrant of the brain—the area associated with social interactions and relationships—is a much brighter shade of yellow in the second scan than in the first. This would indicate much higher uses of this area of the brain than was shown in the first scan."

Tracy then brought up two more sets of brain scans. "Here we have two sets of brain scans for Crow and Green. As you can see, Green has little to no activity in that area of her brain, and Crow shows only a slight increase in this area of his brain from the initial scan."

Tracy's heart skipped a beat as she saw Crow's brain scan. The scientific evidence before her showed that the pilot was starting to build a relationship with someone, and she immediately thought of her recent interactions with Crow. She decided that now was not the time to psychoanalyze herself, and she continued, "The pilots' abilities to engage in relationships with other people extends to the ROCs through the neuro-link. As I said before, the pilots are better able to sync with the ROCs and form a stronger connection between the ROCs' skills and their own when they have strengthened the interpersonal functions within their brains. The feelings that Munroe and Bixby have for each other also seem to be extended to their ROCs as well."

She pulled up footage of the battle between the ROCs and The Loch Ness Monster. "See how the ROCs are helping and supporting each other in the way they are attacking the monster? While these actions are driven by Munroe's and Bixby's cognitive process, they are enhanced through the ROCs' reflexes. See how their movements are supporting each other and helping to keep the other from being injured? These movements are being carried out at a speed far too great to be the result of the pilots' thought processes. I believe that the ROCs are connecting with the feelings that Munroe and Bixby have for each other, and that they projecting those feelings onto each other. In other words, ROC Two and ROC Four are working to protect each other as Munroe and Bixby would do in a battle situation, but they are doing it with the speed and strength of a ROC."

She moved her slide to a picture of the West Coast. "I suggest that we position ROC Two and ROC Four in Northern California where they will be able to quickly address the next attack from the Sasquatch."

Mackenzie cut in, "So you are suggesting that we leave the entire East Coast, including places like New York and Washington, D.C. open to attack from the Lizard Man, who is currently swimming around the Atlantic Ocean?"

Tracy gave a sarcastic smile. "Again, I am not a military expert, but I can tell you that ROC Two and ROC Four will function much better if they are together. I also know that the Lizard Man is in the Atlantic Ocean, and it could appear anywhere in North America, South America, Europe, or Africa. Certainly Rol-Hama has shown that the entire world is his target. I would think that we could mass our Navy and Airforce along the East Coast since we know that the Lizard Man will have to come out of the ocean to attack. The Sasquatch, on the other hand, has retreated to the woods twice already, and he has shown no signs that he is capable of crossing an ocean. So another attack from the Sasquatch seems likely."

Tracy looked to Jillian Crean. "I will defer to Dr. Crean on this point, but the Sasquatch seems too powerful for either of our ROCs to defeat alone. What do you think, Dr. Crean?"

Jillian Crean stood. "Based on the videos that I have watched from the Sasquatch's attacks and his battle with ROC One, I would concur with Dr. Curry. I do not think that either of our ROCs will be able to defeat the Sasquatch alone."

The President cut in, "Mackenzie, I agree with the suggestions of the doctors. We are sending ROC two and ROC Four to California to battle the Sasquatch. I will have as much naval power as possible put into action off the East Coast, so that if we see the Lizard Man, hopefully we can stop him before he comes ashore. Moving on, now that we have Rol-Hama's location, how do you suggest that we proceed in taking him out, and will doing so put an end to the threat of the giant monsters that we are facing?"

Mackenzie pulled up a schematic of the coordinates that Crow had divulged from the cultist that he had interrogated. "Rol-Hama is currently hiding in the tribal region of Pakistan. He has chosen this area for his base of operations, because he knows that it would be difficult both politically and from a tactical approach for us to attack him here. The government of Pakistan would not be happy if we were to send a full-out assault into their country, no matter the danger to the rest of the world, but given the circumstances, the UN should support unanimously should we decide to send the armed forces into Pakistan. The other point to consider, is that while the satellite pictures are not showing anything, we suspect that Rol-Hama has at least one kaiju cryptid protecting his base. If this is true, then even an all assault by the military would probably be turned away by the monster."

Mackenzie brought up a picture of Tobias Crow. "Our plan shall proceed as follows: Captain Crow has agreed to lead a small strike force into Pakistan to attack Rol-Hama. Hopefully, this team will be able to avoid the notice of the Pakistanis and any potential kaiju threat. Crow and his team will attempt to take out ROl-Hama and his followers. The second part of their mission will be to rescue Dr.'s Teig and Branson, hopefully they will be able to tell us specifically how we can prevent any remaining enlarged cryptids from attacking cities. Should Tieg and Branson have already been executed, then Crow will take as many of Rol-Hama's followers alive as possible in order to interrogate them as to the means to deactivate any remaining cryptid kaiju."

Tracy Curry's heart sped up as a Mackenzie was outlining the mission that Tobias Crow was going to be leading. Millions of people had died and the world had reached a turning point of unimaginable proportions, and here she was, one of the top minds on the planet, concerned with the life of the strong, quite, unattainable guy. At first she felt ashamed of herself, as if she was a school girl with a crush, but then she reminded herself that it was the forming of a relationship between Munroe and Bixby that had made them more powerful and had taken a big step toward ending Rol-Hama's reign of terror. In this instance, the power of love was literally overcoming the power of hate. Tracy was beginning to realize that her feelings were not as trivial as she had thought. Whether the world was ending or changing, now was not time to let a potential lost love go off to face a monster without expressing her feelings to him. In fact, now was absolutely the time that she should act on her feelings. Tracy resigned herself that as soon as the meeting was over that she would go to Tobias and express her feelings for him, and she would move forward from there based on his reaction. With her mind made up, she refocused her attention on Mackenzie's briefing.

Mackenzie pulled up a map of the Pacific Northwest. "While the team is en route to Pakistan, ROC Two and ROC Four will search the woodlands of the Pacific Northwest for the Sasquatch. Even with his size, finding him in these forests will be difficult, but if there's any chance of having the ROCs engage the kaiju outside of a populated area, we need to take it. Once the threat of the Sasquatch has been eliminated, the ROCs will fly at top speed to Pakistan to provide support to Captain Crow's team. Their flight pattern will also take them over the East Coast and the Atlantic Ocean. If the giant Lizard Man should attack the East Coast the ROCs will respond to the threat, and should he be spotted out at sea, the ROCs will also attempt to engage the cryptid away from a populated area. The best case scenario will have Rol-Hama's control over the Lizard Man ended before it emerges from the ocean. If Rol-Hama is no longer in control of the Lizard Man, we can decide how to best handle him based on the monster's actions. God willing, the beast will inhabit some niche in a secluded area of the world where his impact is minimal, and then he can live out his life in peace. If not, then the ROCs will track him down as well."

Mackenzie's face took on a look of grim determination. "In short, it is time we stop reacting to threats, and we start taking the fight to Rol-Hama."

CHAPTER 24

Bixby looked Munroe directly in the eyes as he made love to her. The two lovers had sex dozens of times before, but this time it was different. Like the kiss that they had shared after defeating the Loch Ness Monster, this was more than just a physical response to sharing a mind with a kaiju. This time there was an emotional attachment to another human being involved in the process.

When it was over Munroe didn't quickly jump out of bed and head back to her room. She stayed with Bixby, and she whispered, "I love to you." to the young pilot, and then she held onto him as she drifted off to sleep.

Bixby held Munroe tight in his arms as she dozed off. After all of the death and destruction that he had witnessed over the past couple of weeks, holding Munroe was like finding an oasis of peace and rest in a world of turmoil. No matter what they faced in the coming days, whether it be a giant Sasquatch, a colossal Lizard Man, a crazed terrorist, or any crazy threat, Bixby was confident that with the ROCs and Munroe at his side that no challenge was too great. With his mind and his emotions finally at ease with each other, Bixby closed his eyes and fell asleep while holding onto that which was most precious to him.

Crow pulled on the bar that was suspended in his room, and as his chin reached the bar, he whispered, "One hundred." Sweat poured off his body, and his arms felt as though they were on fire. Tobias Crow knew that he should stop doing chin-ups and that his body was already close to its limits, but none of those things mattered. He was not working out to improve his body, he was doing it punish himself for failing in his mission. Crow was not the kind of man who looked at others or outside influences to explain his failures.

He knew that he had failed to defeat the Sasquatch because he was not able to properly utilize ROC 1. His failure had cost hundreds of thousands of people their lives, and millions more, their homes. In Crow's mind, he knew that the destruction of San Diego and every life that the Sasquatch took from this point on would fall on his head. To further add to Crow's emotional turmoil with the death of ROC 1, there would be no opportunity for him to rectify his mistake. He would never have the chance to engage the Sasquatch in battle again. While the lives of the people who had died at the hands of the man-beast tore apart his soul, the thought that the Sasquatch had defeated him weighed heavily on his pride.

Against the protests of his arms, he forced them to continue to lift his body until his face was parallel with the bar. As Crow examined his battle with the Sasquatch, he knew that there were two key factors that led to his defeat by the monster and the death of ROC 1. The first factor was a lack of both focus and execution. Crow slowly pulled his body up to the top of the bar one last time before his arms finally gave way, and he fell to the floor.

Without the ability to exert his body any further, Crow was left with his thoughts. He knew that his lack of focus, and therefore lack of execution, came from his recently discovered feelings for Tracy Curry. What he was unsure of was if it was his inability to suppress his emotion or his unwillingness to accept them that had caused him to fail. Throughout his life Crow had been focused on doing what he had to do, on getting the job done. Sure, he had sex with dozens of woman, but that was nothing more than a workout for him, stress relief, a way to better keep his mind and body sharp for his next mission. He had always thought that emotional attachment was a weakness that he could not afford. He had always felt that having feelings for others would one day get him or someone else killed because he acted on those feelings and not on his instincts.

These conceptions are what pushed Crow to try and suppress his feelings for Tracy, but as he sat on the floor a defeated man for the first time, he truly pondered if that was the correct course to take. It was obvious to him that both Bixby and Munroe were better able to utilize their ROCs once they had admitted and embraced their feelings for each other. From his own experience, Crow was forced to concede that he felt more connected to ROC 1 when he was thinking about Tracy than he did at any other time.

As Crow sat in his room pondering his failures, there was a knock on his door. During his stay at the Nest only one person had ever knocked on his door, and he was sure that it was her knocking on his door again. As Crow opened the door he saw Tracy Curry standing on the other side. He felt his blood begin to rush through his body, and he felt his heart pounding in his ears. The mighty soldier had been reduced to a quivering school boy by Tracy.

The attractive doctor was nervously playing with her hair as Crow stared at her. Twisting her long hair around her finger was an unconscious act that she engaged in when she was in deep thought or when she was nervous. In her mind, she cursed herself for engaging in such a childish act when waiting for Crow to answer the door.

They both stood at the doorway in silence for a moment before Crow finally asked her to come in to his room.

Tracy smiled, entered the room, and stood by one of the two Chairs that were in Crow's room. She looked at the captain covered in sweat and immediately a rush of adrenaline shot through her body.

Crow looked at himself and realized the condition that he was in. "I'm sorry. I was working out. Just give me a minute to put on some clean clothes."

Tracy shook her head. "It's Okay. I won't be here that long. I just heard that you are going to lead to the task force that is going to enter Pakistan and attack Rol-Hama's headquarters."

Crow nodded. "After the way I screwed up the battle with the Sasquatch, it seemed like that was the only useful thing I could do."

Tracy saw the pain in his face at the mention of the battle with the Sasquatch. She knew he bared the responsibility for the loss himself. Regardless of her feelings for him, she could not let him shoulder that burden as he went on to what could very well be his last mission, especially, when from Tracy's perspective, she felt that she was responsible for the fates of Crow, Green, ROC 2, and ROC 3.

Tracy walked up to Crow. "What happened with ROC One losing to Sasquatch wasn't your fault. It was mine. Just like what happened to ROC Three and Sheena was my fault."

Crow shook his head. "How can any of those things be your fault? It wasn't you who was piloting the ROCs."

Tracy broke down in tears as the emotional burden that had been buried deep within her finally came to the surface. "No, but it was me who put all of you in those ROCs. It was me who thought that it was a person's skills and not his or her emotions that allowed them to sync with a ROC. It was me who missed that Sheena was too emotionally unstable to handle engaging in a neuro-link with a monster. I have doctorate in psychology. I should have spotted those things."

She looked into Crow's eyes. "Still, the worst disservice I have done is to you. First, when I began to suspect that it was a person's ability to build relationships with others that increased their ability to sync with a ROC, I should have spoken to you about it. I knew from your profile that this could be a potential issue for you. Maybe if I had discussed this with you ahead of time you would have been in the correct mental state to better sync with ROC One. Then maybe ROC One would have defeated the Sasquatch, and then God knows how many lives could have been saved."

Tears continued to flow down her face as she spoke, "The worst of it is, do you know what really held me back from talking to you about this? It's because I have feelings for you. God, how stupid is it that the fate of the world is at stake, and because I have a stupid crush on someone, I can't speak up? I have multiple degrees and have made the world's first ever interface that allows two minds to directly connect, and I can't even talk to a guy about my feelings!"

Her crying began to slow down. She took a deep breath and tried to compose herself. "Look, I am sorry to dump all of this on you. It's just that I couldn't let you go after Rol-Hama with that guilt on your mind when it should be on mine. Good luck, Tobias, I have faith that you will bring an end to this horror facing us."

Tracy went to walk out of the room when Crow grabbed her arm. "It's not your fault." Crow looked down at the floor, and then back at Tracy. "I have never been any good about talking about my feelings toward anyone. Christ, I don't know if I ever even had feelings for anyone outside of my family, but over the past few weeks I began to develop them for you. I knew it when I was flying ROC One. I knew that when I thought about you that I was better able to connect with the beast. Instead of reaching out to you and talking to you about this, I ran away or flew away with ROC One. I could have talked to you a while ago about the way I feel. I could have flown ROC One to Baltimore and maybe have saved the lives of some of the people there, but I flew the farther route to try and clear my head. I could even have simply accepted my feelings and allowed ROC One to work with me instead of for me, but I didn't. I simply ran from these feelings like a weakling."

Tracy placed her hand on Tobias's cheek. "Maybe we are both at fault, and maybe that is something we will have to live with for the rest of our lives. We can't take back the past, but we can improve going forward. Let's be honest with each other and with ourselves. Ignoring the emotions in our hearts has caused us to be miserable, and as a result, people have died. Let's not continue to make that mistake."

Tracy leaned forward and kissed Crow, with an unbridled passion, and he returned the gesture in kind.

CHAPTER 25

Pakistan

The heat was oppressive as Rol-Hama sat alone at the center of his base of operations, and he studied the reports from his most recent series of attacks. The cities of San Diego and Baltimore were completely destroyed. Major damage had been dealt to London, Glasgow, Saint Petersburg, and Sydney. His creatures had managed to kill two of the so-called ROCs that the Americans used to combat his efforts. Despite all of this, Rol-Hama was beginning to feel as if he was losing this war of attrition. He had lost nearly two thirds of the kaiju at his disposal and still not one country had pledged their allegiance to himself or Kali. Rol-Hama knew that with each monster that the ROCs slew that the people of the world would gain confidence that Thuggee could be defeated. He also knew that the loss of each monster shook the faith that his men had in their belief that Rol-Hama would lead them to victory and usher in the age of Kali.

The failure of his men to destroy the ROCs' base and to capture the people who created the monsters further enraged him. Not only had their failure ensured that the remaining ROCs would continue to challenge his kaiju but it also meant that the two women who had created the beasts were not under his control. Without their expertise, he would never have the level of control over his kaiju that the Americans had over the ROCs. The situation was made even more frustrating by the fact that the groups he had monitoring the families of the two scientists in his possession were forced to leave their hideouts or risk being discovered. There was now every possibility that the Americans and their ROCs were aware of his location. With that contingency in mind, Rol-Hama had used his limited control over his kaiju to call two of them into the vicinity of his base of operations. One of the cryptids turned kaiju had already arrived and was outside of the base in the Gulf of Oman.

A devious smile formed on the madman's face as he turned to look at the statue of Kali that adorned his room. He yelled as he spoke to the idol, "Let the Americans and their ROCs come! We shall crush them like the pitiful birds that they are, and then my remaining kaiju will destroy anyone who does not swear allegiance to Kali and the mighty Rol-Hama."

The cultist looked outside the entrance to his complex, and he could see the wake of a large creature moving below the surface of the waters of the Gulf of Oman. From the amount of water being displaced, Rol-Hama was sure that the Lizard Man had returned to his master so that he may fight in the final battle between him and his enemies.

The Thuggee leader walked outside of his complex and toward the beach of the Gulf of Oman. A warm wind blew off of the water, and as he looked over the Gulf, he could see a large storm brewing in the distance. The madman was convinced that the storm was a sign from Kali that he would soon destroy the mortal enemies of the death goddess, just as a hurricane destroys the constructs of man. Rol-Hama looked at the water as the giant Lizard Man continued to swim in large circles close to the shoreline. Rol-Hama closed his eyes and focused on the ground below him. He had sent out the command for his other kaiju to come to him several hours ago, and given the speed of the creature, Rol-Hama knew that the beast should be arriving at his stronghold any minute now. After waiting for a few moments, the ground below the cultist rose several feet into the air, and then returned to its original spot. Rol-Hama turned and saw a raised area of sand moving across the beach, indicating that some large creature was burrowing beneath the beach. As the Lizard Man circled in the water, this new creature circled in the sands of the beach.

Rol-Hama laughed, knowing that the displaced sand heralded the coming of his second sentry. A lightning bolt struck the ground, and Rol-Hama smiled as he knew that his monster was drawing the power from the very storm itself in preparation for the upcoming battle.

Several more bolts of electricity arched down from the sky and struck the ever moving wave of displaced sand. With each strike of lightning, the monster grew more powerful. Rol-Hama sat outside as the storm closed around him. As the tempest continued to assault the beach, the Thuggee leader felt assured that the Lizard Man and the creature below him would be more than powerful enough to destroy the remaining ROCs and anything else that challenged his supremacy. After the ROCs were dead, Rol-Hama knew that with these two creatures, and his Sasquatch, that he would bring the world to its knees in supplication to Kali.

Rol-Hama looked out over the sea and focused his thoughts on the Lizard Man. While not aquatic by nature, the beast was more than capable of functioning effectively in the ocean. Rol-Hama accessed the implant in his brain and sent his will out to the kaiju. He instructed the monster to circle the Gulf of Oman and to destroy any ship that he came across—regardless of its size. Rol-Hama was fairly sure that any attack on his base would come from a ship at sea, and he planned to have the Lizard Man end any potential attack before it ever began.

As the Lizard Man began swimming out into the Gulf, Rol-Hama focused his thoughts on the creature in the sand below him. He instructed this creature to create a burrow in a ten mile radius around his base of operations. If the beast detected any movement, it was to attack immediately. Rol-Hama made a mental note to instruct his followers to stay inside until he directed them otherwise. With his kaiju protecting his headquarters, Rol-Hama walked back inside as he waited for the final battle with the governments of the world and the remaining ROCs.

CHAPTER 26

Bixby woke to find Munroe with her arm slumped over his chest and her long hair covering his arm and shoulder. Bixby looked over at her, and as he was staring at her, he was filled with a sense of contentment. Just watching her sleep brought indescribable joy to the young pilot, because for the first time in his life he loved someone, and for the first time he knew that someone else loved him. This was the first time that he and Munroe had spent the night together after having sex. This was the first time that he was able to enjoy talking to her after and simply holding her next to him as he slept. This was the first time that he was able to enjoy Munroe and not just her body. He still thought that she had a great body, but now he realized that she was so much more than just a hot woman. She was someone that made him a better person simply by having her around. She was the person who made it worth waking up for in the morning. She was the part of his life that had been missing all of this time that he had never realized was missing before. Now that knew what he had been missing, he was determined to never lose it, to never lose Munroe.

He watched her for a good five minutes before she finally woke. She saw Bixby smiling at her, and she smiled back. "Good morning, flyboy. I don't know about you, but I am in the mood to go find a Sasquatch and kick its ass."

Bixby wrapped up his lover in his arms. "That sounds like plan for the day, but there is something else that I need to do first." He pulled Munroe toward him, and then he kissed her passionately. Once their lips had parted he looked her in the eyes again. "Okay, now let's go kick some hairy Sasquatch ass."

Munroe smiled. "Sounds good, and I have a plan about exactly how we can accomplish that task."

The two pilots jumped out of their beds, took a shower together that was significantly longer the necessary, got dressed, and then headed down to the ROCs' control center. They had their recliners moved next to each other so that they were in close physical proximity.

Bixby was the first to get himself situated and to engage in his neuro-link with ROC 4. Once more he was in almost perfect sync with ROC 4 as the giant bird took flight and headed to the thick woodlands of the Northwestern United States. ROC 4 turned his head to the right to see ROC 2 fly up next to it. Bixby was staring at ROC 2 through ROC 4's eyes when in his body he felt something grab his hand and squeeze it. With his mind connected to ROC 4, it took him a minute to realize that Munroe had reached down and was holding his hand. He squeezed her hand back, and then a second later, both he and Munroe fell into perfect sync with each other and their ROCs.

Forestry Ranger Tom Gale was in the observation tower of his station deep in the woods of Olympic State forest in Washington. He was so far into the woods that it took him an hour to reach the tower on his mountain bike. It was not an easy ride, but Tom loved doing it every day. The ride through the forest was invigorating to the young ranger, and he enjoyed the tranquility of the forest and the wildlife around him. The ride also helped to wake him up and to get his heart pumping for the long climb up the two hundred foot observation tower. The main purpose of the tower was as an outlook for wildfires, but it also served to help in the search for lost or injured hikers.

Tom took out his binoculars, and then he began to survey the landscape. He didn't have any reports of lost hikers, but in the case of fires, the sooner that they were spotted the more likely it was that they could be extinguished before becoming a real problem. Tom was scanning the tree line when he saw a gigantic hairy form rise up from the trees. The monstrous shape extended its arms to reveal a heavily muscled form. The top of the creature's head came to a sharp point, and then sloped downward to an overextended brow. Tom knew exactly what he was looking at; it was the giant Sasquatch that was being utilized to attack cities in California and then disappearing into the woods. Tom was amazed that the creature had made it this far without being noticed, but then again, the legends that he had heard of the Sasquatch suggested that the creature was extremely adept at concealing itself in the woods.

Tom picked up his radio, and called back to headquarters, "HQ, come in. This is Tom Gale at Check Post Delta. I have a confirmed sighting of the giant Sasquatch that attacked San Jose and San Diego. Over."

A voice come back, "Copy that, Ranger Gale. You are to exit Check Post Delta immediately and proceed back to HQ as quickly as possible. We have specialist en route to deal with the Sasquatch."

Tom thought to himself, *What the heck kind of specialist do we have to deal with something like that?* The Sasquatch unleashed an earth shaking roar, and as Tom heard the roar, he figured that sometimes it was better not to ask questions. Tom slid down the ladder and climbed onto his bike. When he heard the Sasquatch moving around behind him he began pedaling harder than he had ever pedaled before. Tom was determined to make the hour ride back to HQ in under thirty minutes.

ROC 2 and ROC 4 were flying over the forests of Northern California when Makenzie sent them a message through the neuro-link:

Sasquatch spotted in Olympic State Forest, Washington. Proceed to target and engage immediately while it is in a remote area. You already know all of the information about the creature. Take it out before it attacks another city!

ROC 2 and ROC 4 increased their speed to Mach 4 as they flew up the Pacific Coast.

Twenty minutes later, ROC 2 and ROC 4 had the gargantuan creature in their sites as they were flying over the tree line of Olympic State Forest. The two kaiju had slowed their speed as they approached the monster.

ROC 4 decreased its speed further, and then ROC 2 began to quickly accelerate. The Sasquatch turned around to see ROC 2 bearing down on it. The hairy cryptid roared as ROC 2 approached it. ROC 2 quickly increased its speed as it neared the monster. When ROC 2 was roughly one hundred yards from the Sasquatch, it broke the sound barrier, sending a sonic boom crashing into the man-beast.

The sonic boom disoriented the Sasquatch and caused it to stumble backward. The creature was able to maintain its balance, and while it was uninjured by the attack, it was stunned by the sonic boom.

ROC 2 began to slow down after it had passed the creature. It dropped to a sub supersonic speed before it turned around and began flying back toward the Sasquatch.

ROC 4 had to act quickly while the Sasquatch was still stunned. In order to use it liquid nitrogen effectively on the monster, it would need to fly within reach of the Sasquatch's powerful arms.

The Sasquatch was shaking its head in an attempt to reorient himself when ROC 4 suddenly appeared in front of him and began spraying him with a mist of liquid nitrogen. The Sasquatch felt the fur and skin on its arm begin to freeze. The creature roared in anger as ROC 4 flapped its wings, carrying it away from the monster, while at the same time firing a barrage of bladed feathers into the torso of the beast. The feathers buried themselves in the kaiju's skin, and while they didn't cause much damage, they did enrage the creature and keep his attention on ROC 4. As ROC 4 was flying into the air with the Sasquatch pursuing it, ROC 2 flew toward the Sasquatch from behind—picking up speed.

The Sasquatch was still trying to reach ROC 4 when ROC 2 once more broke the sound barrier directly behind the monster. Once more a wave of sound assaulted the creature, knocking him forward, and robbing the creature of its sense of hearing. The confused Sasquatch was still stumbling forward as ROC 2 streaked into the distance, and ROC 4 once again began hovering over the monster, spraying it with liquid nitrogen.

The Sasquatch felt the skin on its back freezing solid, and then cracking and falling off its body as ROC 4 continued its attack. A large chunk of flesh froze and fell off Sasquatch's shoulder as he turned to face his adversary. The Sasquatch put his hand in front of his face to protect it, and seconds later, he could no longer feel the appendage.

ROC 4 sent another volley of bladed feathers into the Sasquatch, causing the enraged monster to once more pursue the cyborg in front of it. ROC 4 flapped away, and for the third time,

ROC 2 sent a sonic boom crashing into the Sasquatch from behind. This time the devastating blow shattered the man-beast's frozen hand and sent it crashing to the ground face first.

The Sasquatch was lying face down amongst dozens of broken trees as ROC 4 descended from above and began emptying the remains of the liquid nitrogen in its throat on the beast. The Sasquatch found that it could barely move as its body was quickly being frozen solid.

ROC 4 had emptied the last of its liquid nitrogen on the beast as ROC 2 descend, and then began to spray the half frozen solid Sasquatch with its liquid nitrogen reserves.

The Sasquatch struggled in vain to crawl away from ROC 2 until its body was completely frozen solid. When the Sasquatch stopped moving, ROC 2 flew into the sky as ROC 4 streaked toward the frozen kaiju.

ROC 4 broke the sound barrier as it flew over the frozen Sasquatch, and this time, the sonic boom shattered the body of the frozen monster into dust. ROC 4 veered off into the sky and joined ROC 2 in the air.

Through the neuro-link Mackenzie typed the next command for the two kaiju:

Excellent work. Proceed to the East Coast and await further instructions.

Once Munroe and Bixby had their ROCs headed for the East Coast they took off their neuro-links helmets. Munroe looked over at Bixby. "That was good plan of attack, wasn't it?

Bixby smiled. "Sexy and smart, an irresistible combination."

Munroe grinned. "We have at least two hours until the ROCs reach the East Coast." She then grabbed Bixby's hand and led him back to their room.

CHAPTER 27

Tobias Crow was in a jet heading to an aircraft carrier stationed in the Gulf of Oman. For the first time in several weeks, he was finally at peace in his own mind. He and Tracy Curry had divulged their feelings to each other. While they really didn't have time for an in-depth discussion about what the next step in their relationship would be, the fact that they had a relationship was enough to put Crow's mind at rest for the time being.

He and Tracy had done little more than kiss and tell each other that they cared for one another. She then made Crow promise that he would come back to her so that they could explore where a relationship between the two of them would lead. Crow had replied that while he was always determined to be successful in a mission, that this was the first time that he had a legitimate reason to look forward to coming home.

With his mind no longer struggling with how to approach his feelings for Tracy, he was able to focus on the task at hand of taking out Rol-Hama and his giant cyrptids. Fifteen hours on the jet seemed like an eternity to Crow, who knew that ROC 1 could have made this trip in a third of the time that it took the jet. He still blamed himself for losing ROC 1 and for making this war all the more difficult to win without the giant bird. When he looked out of his window and saw the carrier coming into view, he nodded, thinking to himself that it was finally time to get back into this war.

The jet landed on the carrier, and Crow was immediately greeted by the ship's captain.

The captain walked up to Crow, and the two men saluted each other as the captain introduced himself, "Welcome aboard, Captain Crow. I am Captain Jeremy Hart. I have spoken to Director Mackenzie. I am to escort you to the team of Navy SEALS that you will command in your attack on Rol-Hama's stronghold."

Crow nodded, and then followed the captain to the briefing room of the ship. He saw a team of roughly a dozen Navy SEALs waiting for him. Captain Hart brought up the monitor in the middle of the room to show Director Mackenzie.

Mackenzie took a quick look around the room, and then began addressing the team, "Men, this is Captain Tobias Crow. He is a one of the main reasons that we now have the coordinates of the Thuggee base of operations."

The SEALs took a minute to acknowledge Crow.

Mackenzie continued with his briefing, "Rol-Hama's stronghold seems to be carved out of a sea cliff in Pakistan that is facing the Gulf of Oman. This is part of the tribal region of Pakistan which would make an approach by land difficult, with numerous tribal warlords presenting obstacles in approaching the stronghold by land." Mackenzie had his display zeroed in on the cliff wall that Rol-Hama used for his stronghold. "The good news is that the Thuggee do not appear to have many large caliber weapons protecting their base of operations, so getting to the entrance should not be too difficult, but there is likely to be intense close quarters fighting once you enter the cavern."

Mackenzie's voice became a touch more sensitive as he spoke to the gathered strike team, "I know that bombing the stronghold would seem like a much easier option, but we need to go in there and come out with some prisoners and information. We have no idea how many more kaiju that Rol-Hama has control of, nor do we know what those kaiju will do if they are no longer receiving orders from Rol-Hama. Simply destroying the Thuggee may cause the kaiju to be more unpredictable and dangerous than they are now. Do you men have any questions?"

Crow spoke up from the back of the room, "Rol-Hama is no fool, if he does not have any weapons protecting his base of operations from the sea, then he likely has a kaiju nearby. What is the status of ROC Two and ROC Four in case if we do run into a monster?"

Mackenzie shook his head. "The ROCs are headed to the East Coast of the U.S. We believe the Lizard Man may still be lurking off of the coast in the Atlantic, and we want the ROCs ready to respond should the cyrptid attack again."

As if in response to Mackenzie's answer the alarms aboard the ship began to scream throughout the briefing room. The alarm was quickly followed by the blasts of cannons firing.

One of the ship's crew ran into the briefing room, saluted the captain, and then informed him of the threat to the ship, "Captain, we have visual on the Lizard Man kaiju. He is under a kilometer off our starboard side. We have opened fire, but so far our artillery seems to have no effect on the beast!"

Crow looked to the monitor at Mackenzie.

The director of the CIA sighed. "I will have ROC 2 and ROC 4 in the air and headed to your position immediately."

Crow only nodded, knowing that even at top speed it would take the ROCs several hours to reach the Gulf of Oman from the East Coast of the U.S. Crow and the SEALs then ran onto the deck. Crow was almost deafened by the sound of the ship's massive cannons firing. He looked out into the ocean to behold a scene directly out of an old Toho movie. The saurian Lizard Man was in water up to his chest. He roared loudly and moved toward the ship as the shells from the ship's cannons either bounced off of its thick hide or exploded harmlessly against it.

Captain Hart stared defiantly at the monster as he yelled for his jet fighters to scramble and engage the monster. The Captain was confident that the power of his ship could slay this monster from the fringes of humanity, but Crow knew the truth of the situation. He knew that the Lizard Man would tear through the mighty carrier as if it were a toy ship. As the ship's jet fighters took to the sky, Crow had to yell directly into Hart's ear in order for the captain to hear him, "How are we going to get to the cliffs where Rol-Hama is holed up?"

Hart looked at Crow in confusion as he thought that now was not the time to engage in the conversation about his mission. "There is a stealth sub in the hull of the ship. It is small. It only fits fifteen people. It is built to carry small teams like yours short distances. The sub will be virtually undetectable as you approach the shoreline. All the weapons and tactile equipment that you will need are already aboard it. Several of the SEAL team members know how to pilot the sub."

Crow turned to the SEALs, and he waved for them to follow him. The SEALs ran after Crow, as he headed to the bottom of the mighty ship. Crow stayed to the outside of the ship as much as possible as he descended to the launch deck in order to keep track of how close the Lizard Man was to the carrier. He watched as a squadron of jets dove at the kaiju and blasted it with missiles and bullets. The monster roared and swatted at the jets as they swarmed around him. The jets' attack was furious, but the Lizard Man continued to wade toward the ship—unimpeded by their attack.

Crow finally reached the point where he had to run through the interior of the ship. He quickly ran down to the base of the ship where he found the sub. There were several technicians waiting in the observation room for the sub. Crow ran into it and grabbed the nearest technician. "We need to launch the sub immediately! We are loading up now. Get us into the water! As soon as we are in the water, run on deck, and head for the lifeboats. Spread the word to abandon ship to everyone that you can."

The sailor nodded, and then quickly began the countdown to launch the sub as Crow and his team of SEALs climbed inside it.

The room holding the sub quickly filled with water, and Crow watched as the technicians that had helped him bolted out of the room as the floor below fell away. A moment later the sub was submerged in water and below the ship.

Crow ran up to the man in the pilot's seat. "Go now! Full speed—get us away from the ship as quickly as you can!"

The pilot did not question Crow's orders. The pilot pushed the sub to full speed and it began to move away from ship.

On the deck of the ship, Captain Hart watched in disbelief as the combined firepower of his jets and his cannons were totally useless against the horror closing in on his ship. Many of his sailors had already abandoned their posts and were making their way to the lifeboats. The kaiju was only about a hundred yards away when Captain Hart officially ordered the crew to evacuate the ship. He was still standing on the deck staring at the monster as it lifted its claw above its head and brought it crashing it down onto the carrier.

Hart's ship was strong, and it withstood the initial blow from the cryptid, but the Lizard Man continued to ravage the carrier. As the monster tore through the bow off the carrier, the mighty vessel finally turned onto its side and began sinking into the water. Captain Hart held onto to his ship as long as he could before falling to his death in the water beneath him.

The crew members who had made it to the lifeboats rowed as hard as they could to avoid being pulled beneath the water from the undertow of the sinking ship. Most of the lifeboats had cleared the sinking ship, but to their horror, they realized that a much worse fate than drowning awaited them as the hulking form of the Lizard Man began swimming toward their lifeboats.

The men on the first lifeboat the monster reached screamed in terror as their boat was lifted up in the kaiju's massive claw and to its mouth. A moment later they found themselves falling in complete darkness as the Lizard Man had swallowed them whole.

In the sub, one of the SEALs shouted at Crow, "We need to turn around and try to help those men out. They are sitting ducks on those lifeboats!"

Crow placed his hand on the man's shoulder. "There is nothing that we can do for them against that creature. The best that we can do is to honor them by being successful in our mission and making sure that no one else will share their fate."

The SEAL nodded and then sat down.

Crow looked to the pilot. "Keep pushing this thing as hard as you can, and make sure that we are clear of that monster. After it is done with the lifeboats, it will look for any other vessels in the area."

The pilot nodded.

Crow made a silent promise that Rol-Hama's reign of terror would end on this very day.

CHAPTER 28

The sub reached its destination roughly an hour after the carrier was destroyed by the Lizard Man. Crow had the sub hold a position at a kilometer offshore until nightfall, in order to use the cover of darkness to help conceal their approach to the cavern that held Rol-Hama and his followers. The crew kept a careful watch on a large sonar target that could only be the Lizard Man as it continued to swim in a large circle around the Gulf of Oman. Luckily for the Crow and his men, after the Lizard Man had finished devouring the sailors in the lifeboats, he resumed his large circle by swimming in the opposite direction that the sub was going. The monster's pattern seemed to have the perimeter of the circle that it was swimming in the Gulf ending several kilometers behind the sub's current position. Nightfall was still over an hour away, and the Lizard Man would circle back toward the sub before the sunset. Crow prayed that the distance between the sub and the Lizard Man was great enough that the monster would not notice them, but he had the SEALs ready to make a quick swim to shore in case the Lizard Man started heading directly for the sub.

Crow and the SEALs sat in utter silence. They had already reviewed the plan for attacking the Thuggee base, and given the level of danger involved in the upcoming raid, all of the SEALs were focusing their minds on their mission. The men knew that the Thuggee would fight to the death when they entered the base, which would make their goal of capturing some of the men alive extremely difficult.

Crow's thoughts had once again drifted to Tracy Curry when the SEAL at the pilot's position cursed, "Dammit! We have incoming, and it's freaking huge!"

Crow ran to the front of the sub and looked at the sonar feed to see a large blip quickly approaching the sub's position. "That's the Lizard Man. He's heading right for us. He knows that we are here."

Crow quickly scanned the display of where the sub was in relation to the cavern entrance used by the Thuggee. He pointed to a spot on the beach a half a kilometer down from the entrance that was blocked from the view of the entrance by several rock formations. "Head there now at full speed. Don't worry about beaching the sub, we will stand a better chance of surviving crashing into the sand than we will being caught in open water by that monster."

The sub shot forward as the pilot pushed the machine to its top speed. The pilot watched with nervous eyes as the large sonar hit representing the Lizard Man crept closer with each passing second.

Crow stared at the front of the sub as if by the sheer force of his will he could make the sub go faster and outdistance the oncoming kaiju. The sub began to tilt slightly forward as it reached shallow water, and a second later, it was stuck on the rocky bottom of the Gulf. The top half of the sub was above the waterline as one of the SEALs popped open the hatch at the top of the sub, and the sailors poured out, followed by Crow.

Crow turned around to see the giant Lizard Man only about half a kilometer behind them. The SEALs were swimming to shore and using the breaking waves to help push them along. Their bodies were cut and scrapped as the waves pushed them over the jagged rocks that led up to the cliffs in front of them. Crow was the last man to reach shore, and behind him, he heard the sound of the sub being crushed as the Lizard Man stepped on top of it.

The monster roared as he saw his tiny prey facing the tall cliffs in front of them.

Crow shouted to the SEALs, "Run along the cliff wall. Look for crevices that you can squeeze into. It's our only chance of surviving!"

Two of the SEALs dashed straight ahead into a crevice that they were able to fit into. Crow and five of the SEALs ran along the right side of the cliff wall, while the other four men ran along the left side of the cliff.

Crow could feel the sand beneath his feet shift as the Lizard Man made landfall, and the weight of his body shook the entire beach with each step that the monster took.

The Lizard Man first turned his attention to the men who were running along the left side of the wall. The beast was not a lumbering goliath. It was a quick and agile hunter.

The fleeing SEALs had had just reached a full sprint when the creature dropped down on all fours and caught them in two strides. The Lizard Man roared at his prey, and then he closed his jaws on the SEALs. Crow heard the men's screams as they were eaten alive. He noticed a crevice to his right up ahead that looked large enough to for him and the men running with him to fit inside of it. Crow sprinted ahead of the SEALs in front of him and ducked into the crevice. Like a group of stampeding bulls, the SEALs followed Crow into the crevice.

The last SEAL had no sooner entered the crevice than the claws of the Lizard Man raked the walls of the massive cliffs. The Lizard Man roared in frustration at his inability to reach his prey. The creature continued to scratch and claw at the crevice, causing dust and pebbles to fall onto Crow and the SEALs from the cliff walls above them. Once the Lizard Man realized that he was unable to reach his prey the beast resorted to its reptilian instincts. It simply laid down on the sand and stared at the men, knowing full well that at some point, they would need to come out.

Crow knew that he and his men had a distinct advantage that the Lizard Man would not account for in ROC 2 and ROC 4. By Crow's calculations, the two ROCs were less an hour away from his current position. There was no doubt in Crow's mind that the two ROCs would be able to handle the Lizard Man. Then with the two ROCs supporting them from the air, Crow was sure that he and the SEALs would be able to take Rol-Hama's stronghold.

Then in a flash all of Crow's thoughts about how the upcoming battle would play itself out were crushed before his eyes. From his position in the crevice, Crow watched as the other three SEALs crept out of their crevice and were making their way to the cavern that served as the opening to Rol-Hama's base. The men were sprinting across the beach when Crow saw a long, thick, line of raised sand darting after them.

The men were about thirty meters from the entrance to the cavern when the raised line of sand reached them. Multiple bolts of lightning shot out from the sand and electrocuted the men were they stood. Crow watched in horror as a long, segmented body breached the sand and stretched into the sky. Crow estimated that the portion of the body that he saw was at least two hundred feet high. The colossal worm opened its mouth to reveal a circular row of serrated teeth. The worm dove down on the corpses of the deceased men and devoured them. The worm slithered along the beach until it came up to the still form of the Lizard Man, and then it burrowed back into the ground.

Throughout the entire event the Lizard Man did not move, it simply kept staring at the crevice.

One of the SEALs spoke up, "What the hell was that other thing? Some kind of snake monster?"

Crow shook his head. "I have been researching a lot of cryptids lately. That thing was an enlarged Mongolian Death Worm. The creatures are reported to be able to release blasts of electricity, spit poison, and burrow beneath the sand."

Another SEAL yelled, "The ROCs are on their way. They'll be able to handle those things, right?"

Crow shrugged. "They are prepared to fight a battle where they have the Lizard Man outnumbered. They have no idea that a second kaiju is waiting for them. To make matters worse, they have no idea what the monster is or what it can do."

The SEALs fell silent as the Lizard Man watched them. All that they could do was wait and hope that when the ROCs arrived that they would be able to defeat the kaiju versions of the Lizard Man and the Mongolian Death Worm.

CHAPTER 29

ROC 2 and ROC 4 were flying side by side as they skimmed over the waters of the Gulf of Oman. The speed that the two monsters were flying at was causing the water beneath them to fold back onto itself, creating two long funnels of water that followed them as they approached the beach. Through the eyes of the monsters, Munroe and Bixby could see the Lizard Man lying in the sand and staring at the cliffs that formed Rol-Hama's base of operations. They no sooner saw the creature than Mackenzie sent the information on the creature through the neuro-link and into the pilots' field of vision:

Lizard Man – A bipedal creature with reptilian attributes. There have been numerous reports of the creature in Scape Ore Swamp in South Carolina.

Description – Witnesses of the creature report a humanoid-like creature with reptilian head, scales, claws, and feet. The creature is reported extremely physically strong and quick.

Information from recent attacks – The creature decimated Baltimore. It is reported to be roughly 285 feet tall and to weigh around 2,500 tons. The creature is highly resistant to injury. Attacks from jets, helicopters, and tanks have all proved useless against the creature.

Munroe and Bixby internalized the information in front of them, and then proceeded to take their positions for the attack on the Lizard Man. They had planned to use the same strategy they had utilized to slay the Sasquatch. Munroe would use ROC 2 to create sonic booms to stun the creature, and then Bixby would attack with ROC 4 while the monster was recovering. ROC 4 reduced speed and fell back while ROC 2 rushed forward, quickly approaching the speed of sound.

The vibrations that ROC 2's increase in speed caused traveled far quicker through water and earth than then did through the air. The vibrations reached the beach of the shoreline before ROC 2 itself reached the slim strip of sand that constituted the beach.

Deep in the sand of the shoreline, the Mongolian Death Worm felt the vibrations of the advancing ROC 2. The monstrous worm turned and began heading toward the approaching vibrations in preparation for its next meal.

ROC 2 was closing in on the Lizard Man, when through the neuro-link, Munroe noticed a distortion on the sand moving directly toward ROC 2. Before ROC 2 could a react, a bolt of electricity streaked out of the sand and struck the giant bird. The shock caused ROC 2 to lose control of its flight pattern and crash into the steep face of the cliffs at the back of the beach.

ROC 2 lifted its head off the beach as the Mongolian Death Worm rose out of the sand next to it and sprayed the colossal bird's face with a green poison. The poison blinded ROC 2 and burned its mouth and nose. ROC 2 screeched in pain and then tried to stand, but the Death Worm began to wrap its large body around ROC 2 like a constrictor snake.

Bixby saw that ROC 2 was in trouble, and he urged ROC 4 to increase speed and attack the Death Worm before it crushed ROC 2. ROC 4 was streaking toward the beach when the Lizard Man stood from his motionless vigil of the crevice where Crow and the SEALs were trapped. The saurian cryptid sprang to its feet and charged at the streaking ROC 4.

When Bixby saw how quickly the Lizard Man was approaching, he knew there was no way that ROC 4 could avoid the creature. With avoidance not an option, Bixby directed ROC 4 to increase speed as it approached the Lizard Man. ROC 4 struck the reptile in the chest with the force of a 747 flying at full speed, but the powerful Lizard Man absorbed the force of the impact as if ROC 4 were a gnat. The Lizard Man caught ROC 4, and then he slammed the giant bird into the surf of the water below. ROC 4 was lying flat in the warm water when a wave rolled over its head, followed by the clawed foot of the Lizard Man. ROC 4's head was driven in the rocky terrain of the Gulf of Oman as the Lizard Man raised his foot to stomp on ROC 4's head again.

The Death Worm was starting to wrap its long body around ROC 2 when Munroe directed the kaiju to unleash a barrage of its bladed feathers. The feathers sliced into the segmented body of the Death Worm causing the wretched creature to release its grip on the ROC. ROC 2 started flapping its wings, and then flew out over the Gulf of Oman. ROC 2 flew just above the waterline, and then it reached down placing its head in the Gulf. Water rushed across its face and into its mouth and nose—quickly washing away the green poison of the Death Worm. With its senses retuned to it, ROC 2 completed a wide circle and turned back toward the beach and saw the Lizard Man raking ROC 4 with its clawed feet.

ROC 4's head was driven once more into jagged rocks under the water. When the Lizard Man lifted his foot again, Bixby had ROC 4 pull its head out of the water and then used the liquid nitrogen in its throat to freeze the water around the Lizard Man's feet. The giant reptile hissed when he found his feet encased in ice. The Lizard Man was trying to free its feet from the ice when ROC 2 flew past the creature as it fired over two dozen bladed feathers into the cryptid's torso. The Lizard Man threw his head back and screamed in pain as ROC 4 used the opportunity to take to the sky. The two ROCs flew a brief circle around the Lizard Man before flying back out over the water to regroup and alter their plan of attack.

Crow and the SEALs were watching the four kaiju battle from within the crevice. As the ROCs streaked away, one of the SEALs screamed, "Come on, now's our chance." The man began to creep out of the crevice.

Crow pulled him back in. "Didn't you see what happened to the other man who tried to run across the sand? That Worm fried them before they were able to take ten steps. We need to wait for the ROCs to destroy those monsters before we make a run at the entrance to the cavern." Crow looked out at the ROCs as they flew away from the beach. "Don't worry, they will be right back, and they will take out those creatures. All we have to do is stay here, wait, and watch."

Bixby and Munroe had ROC 2 and ROC 4 fly a tight circle over the Gulf of Oman several kilometers away from the beach as the two pilots removed their neuro-link helmets so that they could talk to each other.

Munroe first looked over at Mackenzie. "What the hell was that worm-thing? It looked like Mothra on steroids!"

Mackenzie was looking down at his computer as he replied, "My best guess is that it is a Mongolian Death Worm. As you already know, it reportedly has the ability to utilize electric shocks on its enemies and to spit poison. It can also burrow through the ground at a quick speed. From the footage that we were able to view from the neuro-link, we are unsure of its exact size and weight."

Munroe shook her head. "How did that thing know that ROC 2 was coming? It shocked ROC 2 the instant that it was over the beach."

Jillian Crean yelled back from her station, "Worms can feel vibrations through the ground. Sound travels faster through water and land than it does through air, because the air is less dense. It could sense that ROC 2 was coming to it, and then it attacked."

Munroe's eyes grew wide as a plan quickly formed in her mind. "Crean, how long do you figure that it will take that worm to charge up for another blast?"

Crean shrugged. "It takes the average electric eel roughly five minutes to charge up between blasts. That doesn't really help much since we don't know how long the worm originally took to charge up or how its change in size effects its ability to charge."

Munroe smiled. "It's our best guess right? Also, I am pretty sure that a charge like that will have more power in the water than it does on land. Dr. Crean, how do worms fare in water?"

Crean shrugged. "Depends on the worm. That thing looks like and earthworm and it lives in a desert. Have you ever walked through a field while it's raining? All the earthworms are above ground because they would drown when the rain fills up their tunnels. My guess is that an earthworm that lives in the desert would have the same problem."

Munroe turned to Bixby. "We have about three minutes until the worm is powered up again. You have eight minutes to use ROC 4 to draw the Lizard Man as far out to sea as possible. We're going to take both of those monsters out at the same time." She quickly kissed Bixby, and then threw her neuro-link helmet back on, and Bixby followed her lead.

A second later the two ROCs were streaking back toward the beach with synchronized timers counting down through their neuro-links.

As the ROCs were approaching the beach, Bixby saw that the Lizard Man had freed his feet from the ice below him. The reptile roared at the approaching ROCs as they flew toward him. ROC 2 flew well over the Lizard Man's head, while ROC 4 hovered above the creature and rained down bladed feathers into the cryptid. After it had completed its attack, ROC 4 began to slowly fly out over the Gulf of Oman, and the Lizard Man started to follow his prey.

ROC 2 could see a line of raised sand moving along the beach, and Munroe could tell that the Death Worm was burrowing only a few feet under the sand. She had ROC 2 flutter its wings above the ground where the displaced sand was moving. The hurricane force winds generated by ROC 2 sent sand blowing out into the ocean to reveal the long, thick body of the Death Worm. ROC 2 sent another volley of bladed feathers into the body of the Death Worm, and the cryptid shook its body from side to side in response to the pain that it felt.

Munroe looked at her timer and realize that she still had sixty seconds before the worm would unleash another of its electric blasts. ROC 2 landed in front of the giant worm and began using its beak to tear at the skin near the cyrptid's mouth. The Death Worm turned to spit poison at ROC 2 again, but this time Munroe had ROC 2 throw a wing full of diamond coated steel feathers in front of its face to block the attack.

As the poison dripped harmlessly off of ROC 2's wings, Munroe saw her timer countdown to five minutes and ten seconds. Realizing that if her timing was right that the worm was about to send out another electric shock, she had ROC 2 take to the sky. Ten seconds later the worm sent bolts of electricity streaking toward ROC 2. Several of the bolts scorched ROC 2, but the giant bird had been able to avoid the worst of the attack. With her timer now set at just under five minutes, Munroe had ROC 2 swoop down and spray the Death Worm with liquid nitrogen.

The worm's body writhed from side to side as its body temperature dropped. The worm did not freeze to death, but its body was slowed and stunned by the attack, allowing ROC 2 to grab the creature in its claws and lift it into the air. With the Death Worm in its grasp, ROC 2 began to fly out over the ocean toward ROC 4 and the Lizard Man.

ROC 4 was staying just above the water as it continually fired bladed feathers at the Lizard Man. The attacks angered the creature and caused him to follow ROC 4 farther out into the Gulf. Bixby glanced at his timer, and he could see that there was less than two minutes until the clock counted down zero. He could see ROC 2 closing in on the Lizard Man and the Death Worm stirring in the talons of his lover's ROC. Bixby had ROC 4 fire one more volley of bladed feathers at the Lizard Man to ensure that the creature's attention remained on ROC 4.

The Death Worm had recovered from the liquid nitrogen that had been sprayed on it, and the monster was thrashing viscously in an attempt to free itself from ROC 2's grip. Munroe could feel the giant worm slipping from ROC 2's grip, and she directed the monster to dig its claws even harder into the worm in an attempt to hold it for another seventy seconds. ROC 2 was hovering above the Lizard Man as the timer counted down to ten seconds. When the timer hit five, ROC 2 dropped the struggling Death Worm onto the fearsome form of the Lizard Man.

When the Death Worm fell on top of the Lizard Man the two cryptids began to thrash in the water, and then a second later, the water was lit up a bright blue color as the Death Worm unleashed its electrical shock attack. The charge was amplified tenfold by the water, and the shock caused the Lizard Man's heart to explode within his chest. As the Lizard Man's body floated along the surface of the Gulf, water poured into the mouth of Death Worm. Within seconds, the enlarged cryptid's entire body had filled with water—effectively drowning the horrible creature.

ROC 2 and ROC 4 circled the bodies of the Lizard Man and the Death Worm several times to make sure that the cryptids were dead before turning and flying back toward the beach. Neither ROC 2 nor ROC 4 had spotted Tobias Crow or the team of the Navy SEALs that were supposed to be attacking Rol-Hama's base and taking out the threat of the Thuggee.

Mackenzie worried that Crow and the SEALs might have died when the Lizard Man had attacked the carrier that Crow was on, but Bixby and Munroe had no doubt that Crow was still alive and that he would not rest until he had taken out Rol-Hama personally.

CHAPTER 30

As soon as Tobias Crow saw ROC 2 carry the Mongolian Death Worm out of the water, he gestured for the SEALs to move out of the crevice and to head for the opening to interior of the cliff wall that served as the entrance to Rol-Hama's base.

Crow proceeded carefully along the cliff, listening for the slightest sound that would signal an attack from one of the Thuggee or from another monster. Crow was totally immersed in his environment. He was soldier, a warrior, this was his calling in life to put an end to those who threatened others. He was fully aware that the most dangerous threat he had ever encountered was on the other side of the rock wall to his right, and he was prepared to face that threat and put an end to it. When he was just outside the cave entrance Crow called the SEALs to a stop. While the entrance to the cave was dark, he knew full well that there were likely several dozen Thuggee cultists waiting just inside the entrance to attack. With the sinking of the carrier, the Lizard Man pursuing their sub, and the battle between the ROCs and the cryptids, Rol-Hama had to be fully aware that a ground attack on his stronghold was eminent.

Crow reached into his pocket and pulled out a tennis ball. He gripped it in his hand and stared at the entrance to the cave. If he tossed the ball in and there was no reaction, then the hallway was likely clear, and the tennis ball would not create enough sound to draw much attention. On the other hand, if the entrance erupted in gunfire, then he would have some idea of how many guards were waiting to attack an intruder.

Crow softly tossed the ball into the entrance, and a moment later, the entire hallway exploded in gunfire. Crow immediately knew that his guess of about two dozen guards was accurate. Crow and the SEALs took cover behind some of the jagged rocks that dotted the beach, and then they began to fire into the dark cavern entrance.

Deep within the bowels of his stone fortress, Rol-Hama smiled as he heard the gunfire erupt. He knew that it meant the invasion of the enemy into his domain. Rol-Hama had lost the majority of his mighty kaiju. His plan of using enlarged cryptids to force the world into accepting his reign as ruler of the planet had failed. These facts were obvious to anyone who was aware of the situation, but through Rol-Hama's skewed perspective, he still felt as if he were on the very precipice of victory. The madman grabbed his scimitar and headed toward the cells holding the two scientists. Even though his mind was deranged, he was still very intelligent. He was well aware that whoever was leading this attack would be looking to see if he could rescue the two professors. Rol-Hama intended to meet this warrior head-on and challenge him to personal combat. The fate of many wars throughout history had been settled by two sides sending out their greatest warriors to battle each other in order to decide which side would claim victory. Rol-Hama cried aloud, "Once I am ruler of the world, this war will be remembered as the greatest war in history! Generations of children will read about how I defeated the leader of my enemies in personal combat prior to ascending to my position as Kali's avatar here on Earth."

Back on the beach, the ferocious firefight continued to rage on. Crow's team had not taken any losses, and he was sure that there had been casualties to the enemy based on the slightly decreased amount of gunfire that came from the interior of the cavern. Still, Crow had no idea how many cultist were inside of the cliff walls. Even if they had killed a few of the guards more cultists could be running through the corridors inside the cliff walls to replace their fallen brethren. He realized that he and the SEALs could be fighting for hours before they were even able to enter the cavern. He hoped that he and his men had enough ammunition to be able to make their way through the entrance and still be able to take the stronghold itself.

Crow fired several more shots into the darkness of the entrance when the sun above him suddenly went dark. Crow and the SEALs stopped firing for a moment and looked skyward to see ROC 2 hovering over them. ROC 2 landed directly in front of the cavern entrance. It then bent down, placed its beak in front of the entrance, and unleashed a blast of liquid nitrogen into it. From deep within the cavern, Crow could hear the brief screams of men whose bodies were almost instantly frozen solid. With its task completed, ROC 2 flapped its mighty wings and took off back into the sky. A second later ROC 4 joined ROC 2, and the two kaiju circled in the air above the cliffs looking to provide whatever aid they could.

Crow and his men waited several minutes for the last white cloud of liquid nitrogen vapors to seep out of the cavern entrance before they tried to enter it. Crow approached first, but no matter how close he got to the entrance, there was no gunfire coming out it. When he entered the cave he saw nearly thirty bodies frozen to the wall or the floor where they stood. Some of the men were in mid-scream when they were frozen, while others had large chunks of skin already peeling from their bodies. Crow could see that the cavern was brighter on the inside through the use of a series of lights suspend from the ceiling. Crow was pleased that at least he and the SEALs would not be fighting in total darkness. Crow motioned for the SEALs to follow him, and seconds later, he was leading them through the underground castle of the world's most dangerous psychopath.

Crow led the SEALs down the ice covered hallway. He had to step carefully when he was walking over the icy floor. He did not want to slip and have any of his exposed skin come into contact with the frozen interior of the cavern. The cold was so extreme that it would cause frostbite to occur at the slightest touch and tear several layers of skin off. Crow had almost reached the end of the long corridor when a bullet whizzed past his face from his left. He dropped to one knee and fired several times in the direction the bullet had come from. The scream of a man and the sound of a body falling to the floor indicated to Crow that he had hit his target.

Crow continued to creep slowly down the corridor to his left where the cultist had come from. The entire interior seemed to be comprised of long tunnels with few offshoots or intersections. This meant that if Crow and the SEALs came across any more of the Thuggee cultists that they would have no cover. A shootout would be determined by who could shoot the fastest and with the most accuracy. Crow heard footsteps coming toward them. He and the

SEAL next to him dove to the floor flat on their stomachs. Two SEALs behind them fell to one knee, and the other SEALs stood up straight.

As soon as Crow saw the men coming at him from the long corridor, he and the SEALs opened fire. The three cultists in front of the group fell down dead, but the two cultists behind them managed to get off several shots. One of their shots hit the SEAL, who was kneeling above Crow, in the face. The man's body fell on top of Crow as the long corridor continued to be a shooting gallery. Seconds after the firefight had begun, it ended. Crow's team had lost one man, but ten more of the cultists were dead in the corridor in front of them.

Crow pushed the dead SEAL off him and moved the man's body to the side of the corridor. He yanked off the SEAL's dog tags in case he would not be able to come back and recover the man's body. Crow led the team farther down the corridor, until ahead of him, he could see two armed men standing in front of a door. Before the men could react, Crow fired a bullet into each of their hearts. He looked at the door, and then he reloaded his weapon. The SEALs following him did the same.

Crow flung the door open and found that he was standing on a walkway that ran around a huge hollowed out cave with computer banks running along the walls. The back of the room contained an armory, and the cultists were arming themselves. Crow was slightly surprised that they were so unprepared for a battle, but then again, they probably never counted on a ROC freezing all of the guards that they had placed in the entranceway.

Crow and the SEALs took advantage of their higher position as they began firing down on the gathered cultists. The Thuggee had nowhere to take cover, and the fact that so many of them were in one area meant that they couldn't even run without knocking into each other. The encounter was a massacre. In under sixty seconds, Crow and the SEALs had slaughtered more than two thirds of the cultists in the room. The SEALs descend the stairs and secured as many of the cultists as they could before the Thuggee members were able to crack open the cyanide capsules in their teeth. When the SEALs had the room secured Crow walked over to the computers lining the walls, and he looked at their screens.

Each screen showed a different kaiju on the screen. Crow saw a gigantic sea serpent, a massive octopus, some kind of formless blob, and a colossal mer-creature amongst other monsters. The thing that stuck out to Crow was that all of the creatures seemed to be underwater. As he studied them closer, he realized that all of these monsters seemed to be confined to the ocean. He was relieved that these monsters would be unable to attack cities, but he wondered what purpose they would serve. He grabbed one of the cultists and addressed the man in his native tongue, "Where are Rol-Hama and the scientists?"

At first the cultist was stone faced and silent, but when he looked into Tobias Crow's eyes, he immediately knew that Crow was not a man to be trifled with. The terrified cultist pointed to an open doorway that led into another large room. The room was empty except for a small platform that looked like a stage with a statue of Kali behind it. Crow carefully searched the room, and one of SEALs followed him for support. The two men walked over and across the stage, and it was behind the statue of Kali that they found the entrance to the dungeon.

Crow saw the bodies of the two scientists sitting in their filthy cages. Two thoughts immediately ran through Crow's mind. First, was that he would not get any information regarding Rol-Hama's plan from these two men. The second thought was that he would have to tell Jillian Crean and Tracy Curry that he had been unable to save their mentors.

Sitting on the floor with his legs crossed and a blood stained scimitar resting on his knees, was the horrifying form of Rol-Hama. The cult leader smiled as he stared at Crow. "So you are the warrior who has taken my home and my followers. You are indeed an adversary to be reckoned with. May I inquire as to your name, warrior?"

Crow kept his eyes focused on Rol-Hama. "Captain Tobias Crow."

Rol-Hama nodded. "A captain. A man in a leadership position but still one who is on the front lines of a war. Yes, you are just the type of man that it is fitting for me to battle at my finest hour."

Crow aimed his rifle at Rol-Hama's heart. "Release those men, surrender, and divulge any information about your remaining kaiju. Your followers have fallen, most of your monsters have died, and there is no way that you can escape at this point. Your only option is to surrender."

Rol-Hama laughed. "Come now, Captain Crow. We both know that death is still an option for me, and I am still fully aware that victory is within my grasp." Rol-Hama stood. "Tell me, Captain, did you see the monitors in my command center? Did you see the creatures that are still waiting to be released? Would you like to know their purpose or how I command them? Perhaps you would even like to know their exact locations?"

The cultist held his scimitar in front of himself. "I will divulge all of the information that you want on those creatures, but only if you agree to face me in single combat to the death. Should you defeat me I shall tell you all my secrets prior to my death. Should I slay you then I shall tell the men who came with you here that same information. No matter what you may think of me, Captain, I am a man of my word. When I kill you I will tell that man behind you everything that he wishes to know about my followers and the creatures that we have created."

Rol-Hama looked into Crow's eyes. "You can see that this is your only option, Captain. Should you try to take me otherwise I shall kill myself, and my creatures will carry out their operation and bring your world to its knees. More than that, I shall become a martyr in the eyes of my remaining followers. My death shall spur them onto to even greater acts of terror."

Rol-Hama smiled. "Still, all of this is meaningless to you, is it not, Captain? I can see into your mind and soul. Like myself you are a warrior, even without all that I am offering, you would accept my challenge. I can tell that you are eager to engage me in battle, to defeat the man who has been your nemesis. To prove to no one other than the two of us that you are the greater warrior."

Crow placed his rifle on the ground and pulled out a long, thick knife. "Are you going to talk all day or are we going to fight?"

Rol-Hama screamed and ran at Crow. Crow charged and rolled as Rol-Hama's sword sliced the air over the pilot's head. Crow stopped his roll behind Rol-Hama, and then he plunged his knife into Rol-Hama's calf. The cult leader grunted, but he didn't scream. Crow rolled again, pulling his knife out of Rol-Hama's leg as once more the scimitar barely missed the captain by mere inches.

Crow sprang to his feet and sized up his limping opponent. Crow was strong, but Rol-Hama easily had fifty plus pounds of muscle on him. There was also the fact that Rol-Hama's sword had a range of nearly twice that of Crow's knife. Rolling into to attack had been risky but reducing the larger man's mobility was crucial if Crow hoped to win this encounter. Crow had the advantage in speed and agility at the onset of the battle, but now his mobility advantage was significantly increased.

Rol-Hama moved forward to attack, and once more, he swung his blade at Crow. Crow leapt backward, and then he sprang forward before Rol-Hama could regain his balance from his attack. Crow drove his knife into Rol-Hama's ribs. He thought that the attack would have incapacitated the madman. To Crow's surprise, Rol-Hama ignored the pain in his torso, and he punched Crow in the face with force that Crow would not have believed could have been generated by a human body.

Crow was stumbling backward as Rol-Hama kicked him in the chest and forced the air out of his lungs. Crow's vision was blurred, and he was gasping for air when he saw Rol-Hama's sword coming down toward him. Crow shifted his head to the left causing the blade to miss his skull and cut into his shoulder.

Rol-Hama pulled his sword from Crow's shoulder, and he lifted it above his head in preparation of delivering a final blow to his enemy.

Crow moved with speed beyond belief as he sprang up and drove his knife under Rol-Hama's ribcage and into his lung. He then stood and hit Rol-Hama with an uppercut to the jaw. As the cult leader was staggering backward, Crow grabbed the madman's sword arm, and he brought his knees crashing into Rol-Hama's elbow. The move shattered Rol-Hama's elbow and caused him to drop his sword.

Rol-Hama fell to the floor and Crow pounced on top of him with his knife pressed to the cult leader's throat. "You have fallen, now tell me everything about your operation and your plans for those monsters."

Rol-Hama smiled as blood gushed out of his mouth. "Well done, Captain Crow. You are indeed a mighty warrior. As you guessed, I have a half dozen of those creatures, and they are all relegated to the oceans of the world. I had warned you that if the world did not accept my terms that I would destroy it, and with those creatures, I have done so." Rol-Hama coughed up more blood as he continued to gloat to Crow about his victory, "You see, Captain, the controls for those creatures are implanted in my brain. I have already commanded them to begin attacking any and all ships on the oceans. Without the ability to access the oceans, society will crumble. Food, clothing, oil, medical supplies— nothing will be able to cross the oceans. The world's economies will crumble, millions will die, and death will spread across the planet like wildfire. Kali will reign supreme, and I will be at her right hand as it does!"

Rol-Hama laughed for the last time. "The truth begins to dawn upon you, doesn't it, Captain? Those creatures are far too powerful for you naval vessels, and your ROCs will be useless against creatures that live underwater. The world should have accepted my rule. Many more would have lived. Now in death I will have my ultimate victory. You may have killed me, Captain, but my victory has already been assured."

Rol-Hama coughed once more, and then he died.

Tobias Crow was left with the chilling prediction of the end of times from the servant of Kali.

EPILOGUE

One week later Tobias Crow had returned to the Nest. Bixby and Munroe had been awarded some well-deserved time off. The young couple was taking a few weeks to further their relationship. ROC 2 and ROC 4 were also given a rest. The two kaiju were back at the Nest where they were resting and recovering from the wounds that they had accumulated over their vast battles. The ROCs took daily flights lasting several hours each day. The sight of the majestic creatures helped to boost morale of people all over the world as the sight of them gave people a sense of hope and security.

Tobias Crow and Tracy Curry had finally begun dating each other. The two people were still getting to know each other while they were growing both as a new couple and as individuals. They were having dinner together when they were called to the briefing room where they found Mackenzie and Jillian Crean waiting for them.

Mackenzie offered them a seat, and then he began to inform them of the current state of their ongoing struggle with the sea-monsters loosed upon the world by Rol-Hama, "Rol-Hama's kaiju seem to be doing exactly what he said that they would do. They are carrying out his final order and attacking any ship that is on the water. So far the attacks have been on fishing vessels and cargo ships. The news of the attacks has reached the public, but they are not fully aware of the scope of Rol-Hama's plan. It's not going to take the general public long to figure out what it will mean when we no longer have control over the world's oceans."

He looked to Jillian Crean, who took over the meeting, "As you know because these creatures are located underwater, the ROCs are not overly effective at engaging them. The creatures have proven highly resistant to injury through conventional weapons. As such, we need to add a naval component to our kaiju forces. Doctor Branson's family was kind enough to supply us with his research, and with that, we have started developing aquatic kaiju.

With these creatures we will be able to hunt down Rol-Hama's sea monsters and engage them directly. These creatures have been quickly put together, but I still feel that a neuro-link is capable of being used with these creatures." She looked directly at Tracy and Crow. "Dr. Curry, we will need to generate neuro-links for these creatures, and more importantly, we feel strongly that you and Captain Crow should be the two people who link with these creatures."

Tracy had a look of surprise on her face. "Why would you think that we are the two best candidates? Wouldn't a submarine captain be better qualified to link with the new kaiju?"

Crean shook her head. "We don't have the kind of time that it will take for someone new to become comfortable with a neuro-link. You developed that neuro-link so you have as good of an understanding of it as anyone. Captain Crow is the only living person on the planet who has engaged in a neuro-link with a creature that is not currently linked to a kaiju. Bixby and Munroe would have to break their links with ROC 2 and ROC 4 before they could link with another creature."

Crean grabbed Tracy's hand. "We have also learned from our experiences with the ROCs that it's not so much the skills of the pilot that make the difference in creating a link, but it is their ability to engage in a relationship with another creature. We are aware that you two have recently begun seeing each other, and while I loath to push you to move your relationship forward at a pace quicker than you are prepared to, the world needs you to do exactly that. The more comfortable that you are with each other the better you will be able sync with your kaiju."

Crow looked at Tracy for support. He more than had the courage to get right back into linking with a monster, but he was novice at a relationship, and now the fate of the entire human race depended on his ability to do just that. Tracy nodded at him that she understood, and in that moment, he knew their relationship had already taken a huge step forward. Crow looked at Crean. "Okay, we will do it. What exactly are the kaiju that we will be linking with?"

Crean brought up the display. "As I said, we are short on time. We didn't have time to create several generations of creatures leading up to an optimal kaiju like we did with the ROCs. We were forced to use Dr. Branson's formula to enlarge already existing creatures. In this case, we needed to utilize a creature that was an oceanic apex predator." The display screen on the computer showed an underwater scene, and the face a great white shark appeared on the screen. As the carcass of a bull was dumped into the water, Tobias and Tracy finally had something to scale the creature with.

As the bull floated into the mouth of the shark, Tracy watched as it went past one of the shark's teeth. She could see that the bull and the tooth were roughly the same size. She gasped. "That shark has to be at least two hundred feet long."

Crean nodded. "Two hundred and thirty five feet long. We have two of these sharks. That one is the male. The female is two hundred and sixty feet long. They are currently housed in the Chesapeake Bay. With Baltimore in ruins, it made the perfect place to keep them. We have electrical buoys to deter them from entering the open ocean."

Mackenzie spoke up, "Our team has been given a new code name for this mission. We are now the Monster Extermination Group." He turned and looked at the screen as the larger female shark swam past the male. "Ladies and gentlemen, we are about to launch Operation M.E.G."

THE END

CHECK OUT OTHER GREAT KAIJU NOVELS

KAIJU WINTER
by Jake Bible

The Yellowstone super volcano has begun to erupt, sending North America into chaos and the rest of the world into panic. People are dangerous and desperate to escape the oncoming mega-eruption, knowing it will plunge the continent, and the world, into a perpetual ashen winter. But no matter how ready humanity is, nothing can prepare them for what comes out of the ash: Kaiju!

RAIJU
by K.H. Koehler

His home destroyed by a rampaging kaiju, Kevin Takahashi and his father relocate to New York City where Kevin hopes the nightmare is over. Soon after his arrival in the Big Apple, a new kaiju emerges. Qilin is so powerful that even the U.S. Military may be unable to contain or destroy the monster. But Kevin is more than a ragged refugee from the now defunct city of San Francisco. He's also a Keeper who can summon ancient, demonic god-beasts to do battle for him, and his creature to call is Raiju, the oldest of the ancient Kami. Kevin has only a short time to save the city of New York. Because Raiju and Qilin are about to clash, and after the dust settles, there may be no home left for any of them!

CHECK OUT OTHER GREAT KAIJU NOVELS

MURDER WORLD I KAIJU DAWN
by Jason Cordova
& Eric S Brown

Captain Vincente Huerta and the crew of the Fancy have been hired to retrieve a valuable item from a downed research vessel at the edge of the enemy's space.
It was going to be an easy payday.
But what Captain Huerta and the men, women and alien under his command didn't know was that they were being sent to the most dangerous planet in the galaxy.
Something large, ancient and most assuredly evil resides on the planet of Gorgon IV. Something so terrifying that man could barely fathom it with his puny mind. Captain Huerta must use every trick in the book, and possibly write an entirely new one, if he wants to escape Murder World.

KAIJU ARMAGEDDON
by Eric S. Brown

The attacks began without warning. Civilian and Military vessels alike simply vanished upon the waves. Crypto-zoologist Jerry Bryson found himself swept up into the chaos as the world discovered that the legendary beasts known as Kaiju are very real. Armies of the great beasts arose from the oceans and burrowed their way free of the Earth to declare war upon mankind. Now Dr. Bryson may be the human race's last hope in stopping the Kaiju from bringing civilization to its knees.
This is not some far distant future. This is not some alien world. This is the Earth, here and now, as we know it today, faced with the greatest threat its ever known. The Kaiju Armageddon has begun.